MW01145891

Arriving in Time for Dinner

MARIANNE HOLMES

ARRIVING IN TIME FOR DINNER

iUniverse books may be ordered through booksellers or by contacting:

iUniverse
1663 Liberty Drive
Bloomington, IN 47403
www.iuniverse.com
1-800-Authors (1-800-288-4677)

ISBN: 978-1-5320-4842-5 (sc)
ISBN: 978-1-5320-4843-2 (e)

Library of Congress Control Number: 2018907439

Print information available on the last page.

iUniverse rev. date: 07/21/2018

For Mom, who in her way paved the way

Chapter 1

It was a cold and wet Friday night in October, the end of a miserable week. It was already dark, and the rain was relentless. Chiffon reached into the back seat for an umbrella, knowing it was probably a wasted effort. The wind would probably render it ineffective. She was right.

By the time she crossed the parking lot to the door of the funeral home, she was drenched, and her umbrella had escaped her entirely, aided by the wind. She chose to let it run, rather than chase it through the standing water in the lot. Good luck to it then. It wasn't doing its job anyway.

Once inside, she stopped to assess the damage. She was, indeed, soaked through. Her coat smelled like a wet dog, and her hair was dripping water down her face and neck. She headed for a restroom to try to make herself presentable before expressing her condolences to Carol Whittier's family. It seemed like the least she could do.

The restroom was overheated but spacious. She walked through the lounge area. It was inviting, with comfortable plush chairs and a coordinating love seat. The walls were pale yellow and the woodwork white. Ironically, it was the sunniest-looking place she had seen in days.

She removed her saturated coat and draped it over a chair before approaching the mirror. Looking at her reflection, she could see the little waves of steam rising from her clothes and body. Her hair was heavy with water, and the clumps guided little streams toward her shoulders. She unwound the scarf from her neck and tossed it over a paper towel dispenser. She sighed and stepped into a stall.

The rain had run down her neck and soaked her blouse, which now clung to her back and shoulders in ways it wasn't meant to do. She was wearing tights, and they were wet, although it was hard to tell if that was from the rain or from sweat. The fabric was behaving like a second, much less comfortable, skin. The room was so hot!

As hard as it was to get the tights down, it was that much harder to get them back up. Now she was sweating from exertion as well. She turned to flush the toilet with her foot (a habit, perhaps a bad one but a habit nonetheless). Her shoe—a rain-splattered gray suede—slid from her foot and dropped into the bowl.

Feeling light-headed from the heat, she lifted the shoe from the water and brought it to the sink, where she put it before sitting down. She sat for a moment on her wet coat and stood quickly when she felt the wetness penetrating her backside. Sighing, she went to the sink to rinse her shoe. There was no question of trying to dry it even a little. She stuffed some paper towels inside to wick as much water as she could before putting it back on her foot. Looking down at her feet, she wasn't surprised to see that it looked as if she were wearing shoes from two different pairs. It seemed that the shoe that had not taken a swim was not nearly as wet as she'd thought it was when she was crossing the parking lot. She briefly considered giving it a bath so that it'd be a closer match to its mate. But she decided that she'd had more than enough water in her attire for the day.

She straightened her clothes as best she could, then gathered her coat and scarf, folded them over her arm, and walked out into the wide hallway, where it was not nearly so hot. In fact, with the door opening as often as it did, it was really quite a bit cooler. Her wet blouse now feeling cold, she walked toward the room at the end of the hall and joined the line of mourners waiting to enter there.

By the time she reached the guestbook and signed it, the wet-dog aroma of her coat seemed to have intensified. She didn't want to greet the family this way. She left the queue to find a seat among the other mourners, none of whom seemed to be as wet as she was. She could see only one empty chair, and it was, of course, in the middle of the room. She made her way to it, excusing herself to the people she dripped on along the way.

Maybe if she sat for a few minutes, she'd dry some, as well as compose herself a bit. She rolled the coat up into a bundle and stuffed it under her chair. She could still smell it, but at least she didn't have to hold it. She nodded at the man in the next seat. "Are you a friend of the family?" she asked in an attempt to be both social and polite.

"Yes, I live next door to them."

"Ah," Chiffon murmured. "I don't think I ever really knew where she lived. We used to work together. She was a nice person."

The man was nodding in agreement. "She was very nice. She sometimes brought me cupcakes when she baked. I'll miss that. The bringing, I mean. Well, the cupcakes too." He smiled a tiny smile and then looked guilty that he had done so.

She hadn't really been interested in the exchange but thought that he sounded sincere. "You must have been close, huh?"

"We were; she lived right next door."

"Yes, so you said. Well, I'm sorry for your loss." There was no point in explaining that he'd misunderstood the question. Eager for this day to be over, she reached down and pulled her coat out from under the chair and stood. The line was just as long as it had been a few minutes earlier, but it was time to get herself through it.

When she finally reached the front of the room, she offered her condolences to Carol's elderly husband and her son and his family. Nice people—and all dry. When she reached the end of the line of family members, she slipped back into the restroom and struggled with those tights again.

Finally, at the front door, she reluctantly got back into the wet coat and headed toward her car. She was glad that the rain was lighter now; she still had to stop for milk before going home.

As she drove away, the inside of the car windows

fogged over. There was nothing dry to use on them, and she periodically wiped her hand across the windshield, hoping to better see through it. She couldn't wait to get home and get dry.

It had not been a great week. On Tuesday, she lost her job. In truth, it was the sort of clerical position that she considered especially soul crushing. She knew that she hadn't impressed anyone there enough that they'd want to keep her on any longer. She also knew that she'd miss the paycheck but not the job. Ah well. By Thursday, she had arranged for another job to replace it. But if this kept up, she'd run out of other options pretty quickly.

She pulled into a parking space in front of the convenience store and hurried through the door that someone was holding open for her.

Chapter 2

Henry was tall and straight. Prematurely gray, his hair was thick and somewhat unruly, so he kept it short. He moved with purpose and focused on the task at hand, whatever that may be. Tidying his yard up for the season was the day's task. After the summer, he always took a day—always a Saturday—to do this.

His yard was not large, and he liked it to be neat. He had noticed long ago how plant material, in various stages of decay, created unwanted clutter around the yard. Of course, he could not stop the trees from shedding their leaves. But he could—and did—choose not to have any of those big, messy trees in his space. He did have to deal with the leaves that drifted into his yard from around the neighborhood, but that was manageable. Annoying but manageable.

Since it was the last Saturday of October, he knew exactly what he had to do.

First of all, he collected the flowers. Years ago, he'd discovered plastic flowers, and he marveled that not everyone used them the way he did. He "planted" them in the spring, and they lasted the entire season. The daffodils around the base of his front porch were just as fresh on that October Saturday as they had been in April when he put them there—even if they were dirtier. Now he collected them and brought them inside to the bathroom. There, he gently swished them in the tub full of dish detergent and water before rinsing them in a slow stream of warm water. Then they were laid out to dry before being stored in their boxes until next April. Along with the asters, tulips, and hyacinths. Oh, and the lilies around his mailbox.

After removing the flowers, Henry checked the several layers of plastic under the ground cover of brown mulch. That was the secret—preventing weeds (or anything else, for that matter) from growing. It was worth the effort when he came home every day to a yard that looked exactly as it had the day before and would the next.

Working in the daffodil bed, he turned his attention to a section of plastic that needed repair. While kneeling in the mulch trying to determine the extent of the job, he heard a door slam. Without looking up, he braced himself for the onslaught. Those boys who lived in the neighborhood just loved to torment him. He tried not to give them the satisfaction, but they seemed to have an innate knowledge of how much he disliked their antics. As they passed his house on their bikes, a sudden group shriek rose, followed by howls of laughter. They seemed to like nothing more than to startle him and make him scowl. Last July, they had spent the week before the

Fourth setting off fireworks at random times, keeping him awake at night and on edge whenever he was home. There really wasn't anything he could do to stop them, but he wished there was. They were rude and annoying and just a little threatening, in Henry's opinion. *Someone should do* something *about them.*

As their laughter traveled with them down the street, he went back to work. He knew there would be one little straggler trailing the group. Someone's younger brother who—for reasons he could not fathom—wanted to be part of that bunch of troublemakers. He always followed them, probably never caught up, and eventually sniffled his way home alone.

Finished with the flowers and ground cover, Henry moved on to paint. He brought out his can of forest-green paint and began to touch up little nicks in the doors to the house and the garage, as well as the mailbox and the side fence. He found it useful to have all these things painted the same color. Maintenance was easier.

Finally, he washed the outside of all the ground-floor windows. By the time he was finished, the sun was low, and it was beginning to get cold. He was happy this job was done now and knew that he'd reverse everything in the spring—windows, then paint, then flowers. But right then, he felt like his yard was ready for winter.

Inside, he turned the heat up a little and began to prepare his dinner. When he washed his hands, the cut at the base of his left thumb stung, and he remembered his morning walk.

Most days, he walked a couple of miles before going

to work. It was about his only exercise. There were several routes through the neighborhood, and Henry chose a different one every day. It wasn't that he'd get bored if he didn't. But there was a lot to watch. It wouldn't be long, for example, before people began to put out their holiday lights and decorations. He didn't do much decorating himself, but he liked to see what other people did.

In the fall, it was still dark when he left home to begin his walk. Sometimes he would count the number of houses with lights on in them versus the number still dark. What he learned was that before six in the morning, most of his neighbors seemed to be still asleep. After six fifteen, though, the majority seemed to be awakening, based on the number of homes with lights on in them.

That morning, he had taken the route that passed the sad house. In the sad house, they woke early. He noticed flickering lights in four different windows. The lights were the type of blue that suggests a television screen. The interesting thing to Henry was that the flickering lights were all different. It seemed that at least four people were watching four different programs in four different rooms. What he wondered was, If you lived with three other people, wouldn't you want to *be with them*? Henry thought that if he lived with other people, he'd prefer to watch television *with* them, not separately. It seemed sad that so many people were each alone in a place where there *were* other people. But maybe he misunderstood "living with other people," not having done it since he was very young.

It had been cold that morning, even for late October.

He could feel winter in the air and sense the beginning of that isolation the bitter cold encouraged. People would stay inside, stay in places that were lit and warm, pretending that it wasn't really happening out there. When they *were* outside, they were buried under layers of protective clothing, heads pulled down toward shoulders and faces trying to avoid the wind. It was a season that, perversely, Henry liked. Isolation never bothered him, and the cold wasn't so bad if you were prepared for it.

Shortly after passing the sad house, Henry had turned left and walked through a neighborhood in which, in his opinion, everyone owned too many cars. Despite the garages at the top of every driveway, there were cars parked along the street and in those driveways. It annoyed him that he could not walk along the curb after the sidewalk ended; he had to circumvent those cars. Sometimes, after a snow, it was particularly difficult to navigate. But, of course, there had not been any snow yet. It was still annoying to him, though. *What do they do with those garages if they don't park their cars in them?*

Beyond his circuit through the parked cars, Henry had approached the grounds of an elementary school. There were long, low chains wrapped in yellow plastic along the far end of the parking lots. Henry would step over the chains to cut through the grounds to a dirt track through the woods beside the highway. That morning as he stepped over, he was distracted, and his foot got caught on the chain. He fell onto the gravel, bracing himself with his left palm—not the way one is *supposed* to fall, but that's what he did. He cut his hand at the base of his thumb. Hoping no one saw him being clumsy, he quickly got to his feet and walked away, brushing his palms down the sides of his jacket.

He washed his hands again and put a thin ribbon of antiseptic on the cut, covering it with a small plastic bandage. Looking around his small but serviceable kitchen, Henry decided that it would be a good night for an early dinner, followed by an hour or two of reading in his favorite chair and then an early bedtime. His life was good, he thought. He did what he wanted, when he wanted, and answered to no one. And that pleased him.

The secret, Henry was sure, was to be organized. His days consisted of long checklists and occasional free time. Go to work. Check. Take a lunch break and eat what he brought. Check. Even weekends could be organized. He'd proven that with his yard maintenance. His checklist applied to everything.

Neighborhood barbecue.

Appointment with the dentist.

Have his car's oil changed.

Visit his mother.

Check. Check. Check. And check.

Occasionally, something or someone interfered with his plans. Just this past Friday, he had run into a convenience store to pick up some milk. He preferred 2 percent in an opaque container.

It could have gone either way. She *did* walk through the door ahead of him. But he *did* hold the door for her, or he would have been inside first. In any case, she reached for the last container of *his* milk in the dairy case. She looked up and could see immediately that he had wanted it too. She looked like she hadn't slept in days and was angry about it, ready for a fight. Her eyes dared him to object. He started to speak but stopped because of those eyes. He was intimidated, and now he was also angry.

One more time, he had thought. *One more time I let myself be taken advantage of by a stranger who couldn't care less about me or anyone else. She probably has a cat, and the milk is for Fluffy. Who cares that an actual human being needed it!* Okay, maybe he didn't *need* the milk, but jeez. A cat? Maybe he was wrong about that, though. She had *smelled* like a wet dog. And that was when he realized that he had run into this stranger twice within the hour.

Chapter 3

Stan disconnected the call and put the phone down on the counter just as Carrie walked into the kitchen.

"Something wrong?" she asked as she moved past him toward the oven.

"Nope. Nothing wrong." He smiled at her.

"Good. I don't want anything to hurt your appetite. Dinner's just about ready." She leaned toward the doorway and called, "Kids! Dinner!"

"Smells great," he said in the quiet of the room before the noise descended on them. It still amazed him that two small people could create such a racket.

"Stand back! Coming through! Outta the way!" Carrie laughed as she brought the lasagna to the table. "If I drop this, we'll all be very unhappy!" She placed the glass dish on a trivet and took a moment to admire it with a deep inhalation. "Okay, we're ready," and she waved her arm through the air toward the four chairs surrounding the table.

Two of the chairs scraped across the floor as

six-year-old Carson and nine-year-old Sunny pulled them out, continuing their loud discussion.

"It was *my* turn. You were supposed to wait!"

"Was not! You took two turns in a row, so I should get two in a row!"

"No, I didn't! I had to skip one when I slept at the Turners' house. *You* had two in a row *then*!"

"All right! Enough!" Stan shouted. They were loud, but he could still be louder. For good measure, he added a shrill whistle.

Sunny put her hands over her ears. "I hate it when you do that, Dad."

"Well, I don't much like all this yelling between you and your brother." Now that it was quieter, he smiled and reached for his water glass. "You two *do* realize that you're part of the same family, right?"

Sensing an opening, Carson began, "Well, she—" But he got no further before Stan's hand was up in the air, signaling a halt.

"Nope. Not gonna discuss it. Dinnertime is something I look forward to, and I *won't* look forward to it if it means arguments, especially about things I didn't do myself. Now—just *smell* that lasagna! Who's ready to eat?"

Both kids grinned at him, and Carrie began to serve the dish. "I don't for the life of me know how you manage to get away with that," she said, smiling. "I get drawn into every battle they have, and it takes forever to get to the end of one of them. But you, you can turn it off like a faucet!"

He shrugged, blowing lightly on his fingertips. "Magic

touch, baby, magic touch." The kids laughed along with Carrie.

That reminded Carson of something he saw in an animated program they'd watched the night before, and he and Sunny began to retell the story to their parents, but they both giggled so much that they couldn't get through it. In their words and giggles, they tripped over each other, and Carrie smiled across the table at Stan. Their eye contact said that they were enjoying this as much as they always did. *It all gets better when I get home,* Stan thought.

They cleared the table when they were finished and decided that the dishes could wait. They'd promised the kids that they'd all walk Trex to the dog park together. The dog was originally T-Rex, named during Carson's dinosaur period a couple of years earlier. When the reminder postcards from the veterinary practice began to arrive addressed to "Trex," it became a joke and stuck. He was Trex forever after.

It wasn't a long walk, and the kids danced and skipped along with Trex toggling between them. Stan and Carrie followed, their little fingers linked, almost holding hands. It was cool, and he wanted to zip his jacket, but he was reluctant to lose the connection between them, even for a moment. He inhaled deeply, letting the crisp fall air fill his lungs. It didn't get any better than this for Stan. His heart was so full he thought it would burst whenever he looked at his family. It didn't matter what they were doing or where they were; he loved being among them.

They reached the dog park just behind Snowman, Trex's best dog friend. The two dogs took off at a run, and Carson and Sunny went to greet some of the other dogs, slowly and carefully as they'd been taught. Knowing that everyone was confined to the park, Carrie and Stan leaned against the fence by the gate, elbows resting on a crossbeam. They watched the fun in comfortable silence, occasionally calling out reminders to the kids.

Sometimes Stan wondered how he was so lucky. He'd met Carrie and known almost immediately that he wanted to be with her forever. His devotion never wavered, and he was confident that hers was as true. He'd never felt that way in his first marriage. With Carrie, though, they hadn't been kids themselves when they met, and Carrie was a few years younger than Stan. By the time Sunny was born, people sometimes wondered if Stan was her grandfather. But he never minded when that happened. He felt so fortunate to have her at all.

"How's Chiffon doing?" Carrie asked quietly. He sensed the tension in her voice. Just last week, he had surprised her by telling her that he'd hired Chiffon. It had not been an easy conversation. He was still struggling to make the deli support them, and now he had added the responsibility of an employee.

"Fine." He nodded for emphasis. "She's doing fine. I think this may turn out to be a very good move."

She was silent for a minute before continuing, "I still don't understand how this can work, Stan. I have to tell you that I'm worried. I just prepaid the karate school through the end of the year to get a discount, and with Christmas coming ..." She paused to take a breath. He reached for her hand and gripped it tightly.

"Carrie, it's going to be okay. I told her I'd think about it when she called to say she'd lost her job and was wondering if I knew anyone who was hiring. The more I thought about it, the better the idea seemed. I mean, I've been trying to attract a downtown lunch crowd, and I think she could help. You know how much everyone likes her, right?"

Carrie smiled and nodded.

Stan continued, "She'll attract customers just by being herself. And if that works, I'll need extra hands at midday. That kind of customer base would be on the clock, and service would have to be quick and reliable. And," he paused, realizing that he was growing increasingly enthusiastic about the idea, "it might even give me an opportunity to get to some of those afternoon soccer games and karate classes. You know how much it bothers me that I can never be there."

They were both quiet for a minute before Carrie said, "I hope, for all of our sakes, that you're right. I worry about money all the time now, as it is. I'm not excited about having reasons to worry more."

"I know you do," Stan hastened to say, "and I wish you didn't. I know the whole deli thing worries you, but I really believe I can make it work. And with Chiffon's help, it might all come together sooner than I expected. This could be the best thing that could have happened right now." He offered her his most reassuring smile. They both knew that he preferred to do all the worrying for the family.

She patted his arm lightly. "You're a soft touch, you

know? You think you can take care of everybody. And you can be remarkably convincing. I hope you know what you're doing, and I'm proud of you no matter what happens."

"I know what I'm doing. And nothing bad will happen. Magic touch, remember?"

The walk home was slower, Trex and the kids having happily tired themselves.

"School night," Carrie said, taking charge as they walked. "When we get inside, Carson, straight up to the shower, and, Sunny, finish that homework."

"What about Dad?" Sunny inquired. "Doesn't he have to do anything?" She made a face at him.

"Wait a minute!" Stan said, trying to look wounded. "Why would you want to turn the spotlight on me when your mother starts issuing orders?"

"Oh, he has jobs to do. As I recall, we left the dinner dishes in the sink, for starters."

"See what you've done? I'll get you back, you know. You won't see it coming, but I'll get you!" He reached for Sunny's hood and gave it a tug, getting a laugh from all of them.

Chapter 4

Stan's Deli boasted "Fresh Soups Daily!" and occupied the middle space in a strip mall just outside of a busy office district in Silverton, Connecticut. It was a single, large room, narrow but deep, with a counter running across the front part of it. There were marks on the floor along one side of the counter that suggested stools may have once sat there. Someone had removed them before Stan took over the premises a year ago.

At one end of the counter was the cash register and a clear case that displayed a variety of pastries. The rest of the counter offered an array of utensils, condiments, and newspapers. A sign affixed to the edge of the countertop read: "Make Yourself at Home!"

A wall with a service window and a doorway separated the front of the store from the kitchen. Some mismatched tables and chairs filled the space between the counter and the row of windows that faced the street. The floor and furniture were worn with age but were always clean and inviting. Stan was a stickler for cleanliness in his store.

On the Monday following the wake, Henry went straight to the deli after work. It was what he always did on Monday. And Friday. He bought his dinner at the deli two nights a week. He bought soup and a dinner roll and took it home to eat by himself. He felt good when he sat in his kitchen with the soup and knew that he had checked everything off the day's list. Afterward, he'd have ice cream (with a few blueberries when they were in season) for dessert. He didn't enjoy cooking and found this a good arrangement for himself.

Even though he generally ordered the same thing every time, he made a show of scanning the menu posted on the wall behind the counter. It was painted on a very large sheet of plywood and was an exact duplicate of the printed paper menus that stood in a Lucite box on the counter. He liked that they were exact copies of each other.

His eyes drifted down from the menu to Stan, the owner, when he was ready to order. But it wasn't Stan waiting for his order. Instead, the counterperson looked remarkably like last week's milk thief. As she stared at him, their eye contact said it all. Both felt wrongly accused of something even though not a word had been spoken. Stan stuck his head out from the kitchen just then and said, "Hey, Henry. Meet Chiffon. You'll be seeing a lot of her in the future. She's helping me out here for a while."

Henry considered Stan his "own" counterperson and asked worriedly, "You going somewhere, Stan?"

"Naw," Stan replied as he headed back into the

kitchen. "But I wouldn't mind having a little time off once in a while."

Chiffon? Seriously? Henry thought. But he only stumbled slightly over the words as he ordered his soup. He didn't like change but supposed that he'd have to put up with this since he had no claim on Stan.

Henry's first impression of her in the convenience store had been that she was tall and imposing. But now she looked almost small. Her hair last week had been loose and wild, big blonde waves dripping softly onto her coat. Today, she had tamed it into a braid at the base of her neck. But those eyes! Those eyes still dared him to challenge her. And he was still intimidated by them.

Suddenly, she smiled, and her expression changed so quickly and so completely that he didn't know how to respond. The smile involved her whole face, and Henry now wondered how he could have found her to be anything other than friendly. He frowned, thinking that anyone so changeable must be unpredictable, and that meant dangerous, in his book.

Chapter 5

“Hey, honey. Haven’t met *you* yet, have I? I’m a regular customer here, so we’ll be seeing a lot of each other, if you last.” The man leaned across the counter to pat Chiffon’s arm.

He was big and loud. He wore the uniform of a local oil company, with his name and the company logo on the right-hand side of his navy-blue jacket. A gray shirt and navy trousers completed the outfit. His shoes were heavy black ones that scuffed the floor when he crossed it, but he didn’t seem to notice.

She didn’t like the implications of “if you last” very much. And she liked the touch even less. Since this was her first week on the job, she bit her tongue and didn’t say any of the things that came to mind. She just smiled at him and waited for his order.

Not in a hurry, he continued, “My friends call me Big Cal.”

She just couldn’t pass that one up. Sweetly, she purred, “Oh! And what does everyone *else* call you?” She held his gaze, not giving him a chance to look away. Her smile seemed to confuse him, she thought maybe he couldn't fully absorb the slight.

Seeming unsure how to respond, he stepped back from the counter. "Ha ha! A sense of humor. I like that." But he didn't look like he was enjoying it at all. He placed his order and found a seat against the wall, watching her work.

She prepared his food and brought it to his table. She set the tray before him, and he began to eat in silence.

Chiffon went back behind the counter to answer the phone and forgot all about him for a while. But after a few minutes, he called her back to the table. "Honey," he said, shaking his head as if greatly disappointed, "I think Stan there is trying to use up some old bread here. This roll is dry and stale." She couldn't help but notice that the roll to which he was referring had been eaten almost entirely.

Customer service mode took over, though, and she apologized to him. "Let me go talk to Stan," she said as she headed into the kitchen. She wanted to keep this quiet, so she hurried past the steamer tables and stovetop to where he was taking trays of bread from an oven. She leaned in closely. "Stan," she whispered, "is there something wrong with the bread? A customer is complaining that it's old and stale. Any idea what I should tell him?"

"Let me guess," Stan said sourly. "Big Cal, right?"

"Oh, you know him?"

"Yup. Comes in every couple of weeks and always finds something wrong. It's the dance we do. He eats all of it and then complains, but not until after the evidence is gone. Then, to appease him and the other customers within earshot, I refund his money. He always wins, and I always lose, because The Customer Is Always Right. Even when the customer is Big Cal."

And so Chiffon went back out front and refunded the man's money. He smiled broadly and announced, "Thank you, honey. That's very kind of you, and I'm sure it won't happen again. I'll see you soon."

She watched him leave, thinking he was the first unpleasant customer she'd met there. She had been enjoying meeting all the new people and was genuinely interested in them. In her previous office jobs, she had always felt isolated and had no interaction with the public. In the deli, she never knew who'd walk through the door or how they'd make her feel. Customers could cheer her up or evoke her empathy. Most days, she went home feeling better for her involvement with these interesting people. Most days.

Chapter 6

Chiffon was late again. It was the fourth time she'd been late, and even though she was a volunteer, she sensed that they were ready to fire her. Maybe she'd pushed it too far.

She spent some of her free time helping a group that cleaned local waters of the debris that accumulated along the edge. Participants donned like T-shirts and assigned themselves to stretches of shoreline, carrying large trash bags and rubberized work gloves. They collected empty food packages, bottles and cans, all manner of paper, and many other things that they tried not to think about. Like, how did what appeared to be a used adult diaper end up at Jaxson Pond?

Chiffon believed that she was helping. She believed that each person has an obligation to give something back to the world. She believed that even the smallest of gestures is important if it improves the world or someone's life. She believed that if each member of the human community made one extra kind gesture, the world would be a changed place—changed so much for the better. She believed that she was meant to do something good in this world, even if she could not figure out what that something was. She believed that if she stayed patient, the right thing would find her when the time was right. Meanwhile, she'd do what she could.

Although this work was important to her, she chronically allowed herself too little time to get to the bus that transported them to the chosen location. So, the rest of the group was always boarded and waiting when she ran, breathless, to the door. The driver smiled and shrugged his shoulders the first time. By the third time, he was pulling out of the lot as the door closed behind her. This time, they'd left without her.

Momentarily crestfallen, she quickly decided to put in some extra time at the animal shelter. She had that bag of old towels in her trunk; this would be a good time to bring them by and spend time with the assorted strays and runaways that they housed. Why did there never seem to be enough time to do everything? she wondered.

Chiffon often chose her volunteer activities based on a column in the Sunday newspaper. It described volunteer opportunities for various organizations. She always read them and wanted to help them all. They all seemed to support worthy causes and didn't seem to ask for much—just a little time.

They weren't expecting her at the shelter today but were, nonetheless, happy to see her. Darlene Carr, who ran the place but had no title, knew that she couldn't afford to turn away a volunteer. She had learned long ago that people volunteer for their own reasons, not hers. And that was fine with her. As long as their reasons brought them to her door, she'd use what she was being given.

"Chiffon," Darlene called heartily, "am I glad to see you! Do you have a little while to spend in the groom room?"

"Whatever you need, Darlene." Chiffon smiled. She was glad she had dressed for the trash patrol. After all, bathing dogs was at least as messy. "Is anyone back there now?"

"Sharon just left, and there are four more stinky dogs in need of baths. Think you have it?"

"I'm on it," she said as she walked toward the area they had partitioned off for bathing dogs. The concrete floor sloped slightly to the back of the property, creating an ideal runoff area. Chiffon prepared to get wet.

Two hours later, Darlene walked around the corner and found Chiffon sitting on the wet floor with the last of the four, Marshmallow, in her lap. Chiffon was brushing gently, and tears rolled slowly down her face. Darlene turned on her heel and moved on to another task without being seen. Their own reasons.

Chapter 7

It was Monday morning, and Sylvie was happy to be back at work. She parked her car in a sunny spot and gathered her purse and her lunch from the passenger seat before opening the door and stepping outside. She took a deep breath and scanned the lot, noting the familiar cars of coworkers. On the periphery of her vision, she thought she saw Henry's car. But it drove past the entrance, so she must have been mistaken.

The wind was cold and made her shiver. She hurried toward the door, knowing it would be warm and welcoming inside. She pulled the door open and was met with wafts of warm, coffee-scented air. "Good morning, all!" she called in a singsong voice as she closed the door behind her. Karen was on the phone and silently waved her hand in greeting. Two of the mechanics were in a discussion in a far corner of the room and, if they heard her, ignored her. The newest of the drivers, the one with the sun-wrinkled face and the kind eyes, was waiting for her with a question. Henry didn't seem to be in yet, which was surprising because he was usually early.

Shedding her outer garments, Sylvie waved the driver to a seat. "Can I get you some coffee?" she asked the man.

"No. No, I've had some this morning. But feel free to get one for yourself. I can wait."

"Not necessary." She smiled. "What can I do for you?"

This was how her mornings often began, with someone waiting to ask questions or looking for some kind of help. In fact, she could have referred most of them to Henry. But she didn't because she didn't mind helping him out. His was not an easy job, and if she could help a little, so be it.

Sylvie's actual job was bookkeeper, and she was good at it. Henry always knew that he could count on her to find any discrepancy and reconcile any error. That was why he'd hired her. But he'd also come to know that she'd take on other jobs and never say no. She was willing to do anything he asked of her and generally did it well. The other employees had come to regard her as Henry's assistant, even though there was no such official job. Sylvie didn't mind in the least, although she hoped it reinforced whatever job security she enjoyed. She was the sole breadwinner for herself and her husband, Ray.

She had always been someone who took care of things. Things, people, situations—Sylvie could be counted on to help sort through the problem and find a solution. When Ray's back began to bother him, she encouraged him to stop working for a while and let it heal. Unfortunately, the "while" had turned into years and showed no signs of ending anytime soon. But Sylvie had a good job and would take care of it.

She had taken care of things for as long as she could remember. It felt as if she had always been an adult or had at least carried the responsibility of one. As a little girl, Sylvie continually saved her mother's life. No one was aware of it, but without her daily effort, her mother would not have survived. She was certain of it then and continued to be, on some level, even today.

Her father had been a drinker—that, too, went back at least as far as her memory. Sober, he was firm but good-hearted. When drinking, he was bad-tempered and mean-spirited. But for her prayers, Sylvie knew, he would have eventually killed her mother. She'd seen it in his eyes, heard it in his voice, felt it in the air. And so, the girl had prayed.

She had never gone far from home. She needed to maintain contact, lest she forget her charge even for a second. She'd known what a disaster it would be if she hadn't heard every word, known what was going on.

The summers were the worst of all. When the weather was good, he went out every night. As the door closed behind him, every fiber of her body would begin to relax. The respite had been good; she'd needed the time to build energy for the battle that was to come, the one she fought when he came home. The strain had never lessened; instead, it had seemed to grow. She'd worried about what would happen if her strength deserted her—and the fear she felt was for her mother.

When she heard him (Sylvie rarely addressed her

father and consciously thought of him only as "him") come home, she would creep into her bed. Not to avoid him—he'd never bothered (with) her. But her job required concentration. Once in bed, she curled up tightly, slid her rosary out from under her pillow, and began to work with unequalled, unrelenting diligence. While he cursed and screamed and threatened, Sylvie waged a private war with heaven. Clutching tiny plastic beads, eyes pinched closed, she would call on God and demand His attention. She cried and begged and raged passionately. She bargained with God for her mother's life. She made promises—promises she took great pains to keep.

Whether her wordy torrent had annoyed Him, or He'd sympathized with her plight, Sylvie could not have said. But God had always answered her sooner or later. He'd done it invariably by making her father tired. And then her parents would go to bed. But experience had taught her not to give up too soon. She might be winning, but she worked harder than ever. She listened to the voices rise and fall, each peak a defeat and each slump a triumph. Eventually, when he'd fallen asleep and she was sure of it, she would relax her arms and shoulders. If she'd noticed the aching muscles, she never let on. Once it was over, she, too, could sleep.

Sylvie had taken this burden upon herself and never questioned it. It had simply been her responsibility. She had learned at school how to handle the situation at home. The nuns had told her all about God: all-powerful, merciful, and just. They'd told her that He was the source of all good, that she only needed to ask and, provided

He deemed it worthy, she would receive. And they told her that there would be consequences when she failed to obey, believe, worship. She had believed what they taught her and put her faith in God. He could do things no one else could—He could control her father, after all. So, what the good sisters had told her must be true. She was glad to have the benefit of their knowledge and was grateful to them for it. And they, in turn, appreciated her apparent dedication to their teachings. They commented among themselves that she showed great promise. She had potential, they said.

She'd wondered what miracle God worked between them when they slept, for each morning after, both of her parents acted as if nothing had happened. Love was complicated, she thought. *They must love each other because they're married*, she guessed, thinking that was how it worked. And she loved both of them, although differently. She thought her mother was the best person who'd ever lived. Just look at her patience and tolerance! And she loved *him* because he was her father, and she had to love him. If, as she'd been taught, hating another person was the ultimate sin, what kind of atrocity must it be to hate one's own father? True, in some moments, she thought him unreasonable, unappreciative, and unbearable. But those had been vague, fleeting feelings. She could be angry with him, maybe. But hate him? No, never. His only real fault was hurting her mother. A big one—but only the one.

There came a day, when Sylvie was about thirteen, when everything changed in a heartbeat. She had come in from school that day, sensing something unusual, distressing. The house was quiet at first, and she'd stood in the middle of the kitchen, confused. Her stomach sank, and a sense of dread closed in as she realized that he was already home. Slowly, she moved her eyes toward her parents' room. On the edge of the bed, her father sat crying, and her mother had her arm around his shoulders. Sylvie stood perfectly still. Her father tried to explain, but she didn't hear any of it. All she knew at that moment was that, for an infinite second, she felt glad—glad that he was hurting, glad that he was suffering. And then the moment was gone. But it was too late, and she couldn't take it back. Not ever.

Turning slowly, she'd walked into her room and stretched out on the bed. She was calm then, and the numbness began to wear off. She sympathized with him, of course, sorry for whatever was so wrong. But she knew what that infinite second had meant. While her defenses had been down, while she'd been unprepared, the evil had crept in. It had entered, and she knew that it would always be in her.

She tried to talk to God, but He was silent. She tried to explain that she'd been weak but had repented. He didn't answer. She prayed for forgiveness and that rush of strength that He'd always provided her, that renewal of energy that she needed. But He wasn't there for her. The emptiness spread through her slowly, and she rolled onto her side, pulling her legs up toward her chest. She cried bitterly, this time for herself.

Not too long afterward, she met Ray. It was easy to

replace those other two men in her life, God and her father, with Ray. After all, he needed her.

They were so young when they married. Each had wanted to escape something, and they saw marriage as the perfect way. They found a tiny apartment, and both worked for tiny paychecks. It was enough for them to play at keeping a household, and they were both happy for a time.

From the start, Ray had all the opinions and made all the decisions. Sylvie didn't mind. She was sure that, with the right love and support from her, he'd come to the right conclusions. But she was wrong.

Ray liked to be in charge. Sylvie went along with that but began to notice that she didn't always agree. If she tried subtly to suggest that something other than his opinion might be important, it didn't go well. He would demean her, tell her she wasn't smart enough to know what she was talking about. It hurt that he didn't value her opinion, but she learned to live with it. After all, he didn't drink much and never threatened her. This was how she knew that he really loved her.

Life often went wrong for Ray and Sylvie. The car was repossessed, for example. Sylvie was embarrassed; Ray was furious. When the landlord asked them not to store food in the basement, Sylvie understood, but Ray was furious. When Ray was denied a promotion to a supervisory position, Sylvie felt sorry for him. Ray was, of course, furious. These things were, in Ray's opinion, someone else's fault—and Sylvie was usually the someone else. He accused her of taking the other side against him, of wanting to see him fail. It wasn't true, but Ray seemed to feel better if it was Ray against the world.

Everything around them began to fall apart—literally. The dryer stopped working, and Ray claimed that he could fix it. As soon as he had a chance. But since he never actually attempted to do so, his claim couldn't be proved or disproved. He just never got around to it, and Sylvie was still drying clothes on a clothesline as a result. If asked, she'd say that she liked the smell of clothing dried in fresh air. But, in truth, she was embarrassed that Ray neither fixed their things nor allowed her to find someone else who could.

Ray was also fond of belittling her. He'd say something like, "You shouldn't wear that dress anymore until you lose some weight." Even though she liked the dress and hadn't gained weight since she bought it, Sylvie would stop wearing it.

It wasn't long before Sylvie reached the disappointing conclusion that they were not a partnership at all, as she'd hoped they would be when they married. No, she seemed to have signed on to Team Ray, instead.

When he hurt his back, Sylvie thought maybe he'd been hurting for a long time, and maybe if he healed, he'd be happier. So, she encouraged him to leave his job. Take some time off and heal. He could always get another job when he felt better. But he never got another job. And he never seemed to feel better. Sylvie wondered about the cause and effect in that, but it was too late to do anything about it.

As time passed, Ray became even more miserable.

Although he had time, he did nothing around the house. He complained that it took Sylvie too long to get anything finished, complained that she spent too much time at work, that she earned too little. He told her that she was getting old and looked the part. He began to suggest that he'd be better off without her, even though she did everything for him (however badly).

Sylvie would look at the other men she knew and compare them with Ray. She did this not in a "better or worse" kind of way. She just wanted to know what made him so unhappy, so different from some of the others. She thought Henry was a good example of a man who knew how to take care of himself and didn't seem to mind doing it. No one ever described Henry as happy, but neither did they describe him as unhappy. Sylvie wanted to know what made Henry so stable, so self-confident, so capable. Maybe someday she'd find a way to ask him just that.

Chapter 8

Henry and Chiffon tolerated each other over the course of the winter. For months, they conducted their twice weekly transactions in efficient but cordial fashion.

Henry's order seldom varied, and his timing was largely unchanged. He began to grow comfortable with her service rather than Stan's. If only she was a little more predictable, it would be easier for him. Some days she was happy, and nothing seemed to bother her. She couldn't carry a tune, but on those days, it didn't stop her from trying. Unpleasant customers, food disasters, she took them all in stride. Other days, before they exchanged a single word, he could tell by her face that it would take very little to ignite her fury. He had seen it happen and fervently hoped to never be on the wrong side of her wrath. If that happened, he might have to find a new deli, and he would not enjoy that at all.

The other thing he struggled to understand was her clothing. One day she'd be in a long red skirt with blue cowboy boots and a bright yellow shirt, her hair loose and following like a big gold cloud, chunky gold bangles tinkling along her arms. Another day, she'd be in tailored black slacks and white blouse with flat shoes and no jewelry, her hair tied neatly at the nape of her neck. He wondered if there was a pattern between her moods and her attire, but he never could identify one.

This was how he knew that they'd never choose each other as friends. He was all about predictability. His days were arranged for predictable results. His clothes were pretty much all the same; he wore the style and brand of shirt that he found most functional at work. He liked striped, cotton shirts with long sleeves that he could leave down or roll up, as appropriate. He liked khaki slacks that were neutral in color and weight; they would go with any shirt he chose to wear. And with that combination, why would anyone need anything other than a pair of brown shoes? Okay, he *did* own black shoes too, but he rarely wore them.

Not surprisingly, if it was functional, then he also found it comfortable. So why on earth would he buy a different shirt? He never had to think about what to wear. He could close his eyes and reach into his closet any morning, and he'd always be suitably dressed for work.

Stability, predictability—these traits made life easier. They had value. Change, in Henry's opinion, was dangerous. And everything about Chiffon seemed changeable on a daily basis. No, they wouldn't ever be friends. But by the end of winter, their greetings when he walked into the deli had graduated to smiles. That was enough progress, he thought.

He had the vague feeling that she saw him as *too* predictable. She sometimes teased him about his order, pretended to hear him order something unusual. Or she might say, "Wait! It can't be Friday already!" when he came through the door. *One day, I might come on a Thursday or a Tuesday*, he thought. Just to change it up. But he never did it.

Chapter 9

The automatic doors whispered open, and Henry stepped into the lobby. He disliked this building and pretty much everything about it. There was an odor that always, always stayed with him long after he left. It wasn't an odor that they could scrub away or cover up with some sickening floral scent. No, it was just the way the place smelled.

His mother was in room 322. He had been visiting her three times a week for six years now. Why they called it a "rehabilitation" center was unclear to him. At least in his mother's case, this was not a rehab stint. There would be no going home for her.

Her room was, as usual, uncomfortably warm for Henry. His mother looked so small and still in that bed. She was often asleep when he arrived; sometimes she slept through his entire visit. He crossed the room to the chair beside her bed and sat, sliding his hand over hers and covering it completely. She startled, and he was sorry to have woken her. "Who's there?" she asked in fright. She had never adjusted to the blindness that cruelly descended in her later years.

"Hi, Mom. It's Henry. Your son, Henry."

"I don't know any Henry."

"Okay," he said agreeably. "Is it okay if I just visit with you for a bit?"

"I suppose." She sounded reluctant.

He had seen the lunch cart outside the door, and it didn't look as if she'd eaten anything. "Good! Have you had lunch yet?"

"No, no lunch."

"How are you feeling today?"

"Fine. I feel fine."

This was the same conversation that they'd had the last time and probably would the next. He was not a great conversationalist anyway, but it was especially hard with someone who was so disconnected from the world.

"I'm glad to hear that. Do you know what today is? It's your birthday. Happy birthday!"

"It is? I guess I'd forgotten."

"Do you remember how old you are?"

"I think I'm … let me see … I think I'm fifty now. Am I fifty?"

"No, Mom, you're not fifty. You're eighty-one."

"Eighty-one! I had no idea! Imagine that!" She chuckled.

"Yes." Henry smiled. "Imagine that."

"And what time of year is it?" She became somewhat engaged in the conversation, and he was glad of it. "Are there flowers blooming?"

"I saw the first crocus this morning."

"It's spring then." She nodded sagely. "The daffodils will follow soon, I guess."

"I guess so …" His voice trailed off. This was about the extent of their usual conversation. There was little else to talk about, little that she would understand or care anything about. They usually covered the weather, the time of year, and any holiday that might be near. That was about it. She didn't remember much else to talk about.

He was quiet, lost in his own thoughts for a minute. When he didn't speak, she quietly began a conversation with herself.

"Is he still here?

"Yes, I think he is.

"What does he want?

"I don't know.

"Is he still here?"

Henry squeezed her hand lightly and said, "It's okay, Mom. I'm still right here."

"Oh. I see." But, of course, she didn't.

"I brought you something," he said, rustling a paper bag. "Do you remember those cheese Danish from Monterey's that you used to like so much? I brought one for you." Her diet didn't actually include such things, but it was her birthday, after all.

She reached her hand out. "Okay then, let me have it."

He placed it in her hand, and she carefully lifted herself slightly on her left elbow. Without a word, she ate the entire Danish and settled back onto her pillow, sugary crumbs stuck to her face around her mouth. Feeling suddenly queasy, Henry looked toward the door, hoping that someone would come in and clean them off so he wouldn't have to keep looking at them.

"Is he still here?"

Chapter 10

Chiffon was wearing soft-soled shoes and made no noise walking into the kitchen. She stopped just inside the doorway to watch.

Stan's back was to her as he shuffled side to side, a short stepladder in his hands. It didn't move easily on the floor designed not to be slippery. But he persisted. She thought she could hear him humming, but maybe that was the fan over the stove. Stepping to his left, he made a ninety-degree turn and saw her standing there watching. Reddening, he quickly pushed the stepladder aside and cleared his throat. "Are we all set for lunch?" he asked as he bent to retrieve a pot from under a counter.

Grinning, Chiffon moved into the middle of the room, chanting, "*One,* two, three, *one,* two, three. Stan, were you dancing with that ladder?"

"Don't be ridiculous, Chiffon," he said, but the color in his face and neck betrayed him.

"Oh, I think you were. Why? Are you practicing for something?" she asked, unable to contain her curiosity.

He cleared his throat again. "I was thinking about the spring father-daughter dance at Sunny's school next weekend, that's all. Really looking forward to it; guess I lost myself in the moment ..." His voice trailed off.

"Not so sure you're looking forward to it all that much. Are you nervous about it? Because you'd have no reason to know this, but it's unlikely that you'll actually be required to dance. And even if you do dance, it'll be among a sea of other fathers struggling the same way you are. You really don't need to worry about this until her wedding, I expect. She's not getting married soon, is she?"

He frowned at her, saying, "Easy for you to say. I just don't want to embarrass her, you know? She still likes me, and I want to keep it that way as long as possible."

Chiffon laughed. "Stan, she loves you! Nothing you could do on the dance floor is going to change that. Well, maybe if you did the chicken dance ..."

He ignored her and continued, "When she was little, she thought I was Superman, and I got used to that. The older she gets, the more she sees that I'm just a guy. And some day she'll find a better guy. I don't want her to start looking too soon."

Serious now, Chiffon said, "You'll never be 'just a guy' to Sunny. You'll always be Superman, even when she doesn't act like she knows it. You'll see. You'll always be her daddy, and no one will ever love her more than you do. No one will ever take your place in her heart."

"You sound just like Carrie. Must be a woman thing."

"No, Stan. It's a daughter thing. Is Sunny more excited about it than you are?"

"Yeah." He finally grinned. "She says she can't wait to have me all to herself. As if she *never* gets my attention. I hope she isn't disappointed. I want it to be perfect for her."

"If you can relax, I think you'll have fun. I can't wait to hear all about it!"

Chiffon thought she might be able to help make it perfect for Sunny. The next day was Saturday, and it was expectedly slow in the deli. She asked Stan if she could take part of the afternoon off, and he agreed. She called ahead to Carrie and said she had some shopping to do and wondered if Sunny would like to go with her. Sunny was happy to go and was ready when Chiffon arrived a few minutes later.

Although they liked spending time together, it seemed like there weren't many opportunities for that. As they drove, Chiffon asked a couple of questions, and they were enough to get Sunny talking. They talked about school and siblings, soccer and sleepovers.

"No, we didn't have language arts when I was in school. Sounds kind of fun, though."

"Well, it would be fun, but Mrs. Roque is tough, and I sit right next to *Jason*, of all people."

"Uh huh. And who would you rather sit next to?"

"Oh, that's easy. Julia is my best friend, and she's also, like, the smartest kid in the school. And Mrs. Roque likes *her* better than the rest of us."

"Hoping for a little halo effect, huh?"

"What's that mean?"

Chiffon explained what she meant, but before she was finished, the conversation seemed to have taken a turn.

Now they seemed to have moved on to a birthday party for someone named Anna.

When Chiffon turned off the ignition, Sunny finally looked around and remembered what they were doing. Chiffon said, "I have to return a pair of shoes first, but then we can go wherever you'd like. I understand you have a father-daughter dance coming up soon. That sounds like fun! What are you planning to wear?"

"I have a blue dress that I really like, but Mom says I've gotten taller, and it's too short. She's going to try to let the hem down so I can still wear it."

"It might be fun to look at some new dresses here. You know, just in case something is on sale. What do you think? Should we look?"

"We can look, but I know we can't buy anything new. Mom says I'll need new sneakers soon, and she's saving for them now."

"Well, let's just look. I have some coupons, and sometimes I find things on sale that end up costing almost nothing. Maybe we'll be lucky."

Not surprisingly, they *were* lucky and found a dress that Sunny loved and Chiffon assured her was "almost free."

"You look so pretty in that color. You'll get to wear that other times too. It's really a great deal!"

"I guess so," Sunny said. She couldn't quite let go of the dress on the hanger, even though she was protesting, "Mom won't like that I let you buy it. She won't like it at all!"

"I'll explain to her," Chiffon said as she carried the

dress to the register. "She'll understand. And if she *really* doesn't understand, we'll return it, okay?"

When she got home, Sunny ran into the house calling, "Mom? Mom! You have to come see!"

Carrie came to the door, wiping her hands on a towel. "Chiffon," she offered, "would you like to stay for dinner? There's plenty, and I'm sure the boys would like it if you stayed."

"No, thank you, Carrie. I already have plans and need to be heading home soon. I just wanted to talk to you for a minute about something I bought for Sunny." She held her hand out as Carrie began to shake her head. "I know, I know. We didn't ask permission, but it was on sale, and we were afraid—well, really, *I* was afraid—that it would be gone if we came back later. It was such a good deal, and she looks so pretty in it. Please let her keep it! I forced it on her because it looked so good!"

By now, Sunny had it out of the bag and was holding it up against her shoulders. "What do you think, Mom? Do you like it?"

"Oh, honey. Of course I do! That's a beautiful color for you. But we can't have Chiffon spending money like this. She has her own bills to pay!"

"Carrie, it was such a good sale it was practically free. I'm so happy to do it! I thought maybe Sunny could wear it to the father-daughter dance next week. Don't you think she'll be the prettiest girl there?"

Carrie sighed and then smiled. "I already know she'll be the prettiest girl there." She was silent for a moment and then turned to Chiffon. "Thank you," she said. "Thank you for this. If Sunny wants it, she can keep it."

"Woohoo!" Sunny shouted. "I have to go tell Julia! Thank you, Chiffon! Thank you so much!" With a big hug and a big grin, she was off to tell her friend about her day and her new acquisition.

Carrie hugged her too. "You're very sweet, and we owe you one, Chiffon."

"No, you don't owe me anything. Thank *you* for loaning her to me for the afternoon. We had fun! I should make it a point to do this more often," she said, glancing at her watch. "But now I really should run. My best to your boys, especially the one that I don't see every day."

She couldn't stop smiling all the way home. Sure, the dress was an unexpected expense, but the way Sunny's eyes lit up when she saw it more than compensated. Chiffon knew that it had cost Stan to hire her and was happy to find a small way to express her appreciation.

Chapter 11

The next day, Carrie was putting laundry away when she noticed the dress hanging on the outside of Sunny's closet door. She enjoyed seeing her daughter grow up and was pleased that she was looking forward to this dance so much. But she felt guilty too—guilty that she couldn't be the one to take Sunny shopping and suggest a new dress. Guilty that she didn't contribute to the financial well-being of their household.

When she'd met Stan, she had been a dental hygienist and was gainfully employed. Dr. Barnes treated her well, and she had no plans to leave the practice, let alone leave the working world behind. But after they married and she'd learned that she was pregnant, her attitude about a lot of things changed. And one of those things was being a working mother. She and Stan agreed that, as long as they were able to do it, he would be the working parent, and she would be home with the kids. She had thought that, if necessary, she was skilled enough to return to the workforce at any time. But, in reality, she quickly began to see that she wasn't keeping up in her profession, and *going back* would really mean *starting over.*

Carrie was five when her mother died of cancer. To her dismay, she remembered nothing about her mother. Nothing at all. What she *did* remember was how she felt afterward, so very sad. It was difficult for her to explain how it felt to be that five-year-old. There were no grown-up words for it. The sadness mellowed over the years, and she now reserved some of it for the fact that she didn't remember her mother.

The emotions of parenthood took precedence, of course, and she relegated the sadness to a more distant part of herself. The joy of motherhood! It was all-encompassing and so welcome! Like all parents, she could not have guessed at the seismic shift that would take place virtually overnight. Suddenly, the fierce love and protectiveness she felt for this tiny, new dependent scared and thrilled her. And three years later, she got to do it all over again when Carson was born.

She experienced new emotions when he inexplicably struggled to breathe soon after they'd brought him home. His skin slightly blue, they rushed him to the hospital and waited through round after round of testing. Barely able to breathe herself, Carrie watched Sunny as they sat in the too-quiet waiting room. Sunny was looking off into the distance and understood little of what was happening. They'd told her that the baby was sick and then rushed them all off to this waiting room. What Carrie saw was something akin to the sadness she remembered in her own young life. She vowed to do everything in her power to prevent her daughter from suffering the same fate. Not knowing what could be going through Sunny's mind at the age of three, Carrie picked her up and hugged her close. Worried to distraction about her baby, she still remembered that sadness. *Please,* she prayed, *please keep her safe from that lonely sadness.*

In the end, Carson was fine. They had long since stopped watching him breathe as he slept. But that image of Sunny in the waiting room stayed with Carrie.

Now that the kids were in school much of the day, she wondered about what she had given up when she gave up her job. She wondered if she had something to offer beyond her family. That lonely sadness wasn't just hers. Many other children and families had been affected by something like it. She wished she could help.

She did help Stan at the deli when he needed her, but they both knew that she couldn't do that on a daily basis. Nevertheless, she felt some self-induced pressure to do something meaningful with the time she had. But she had already spent too much time in her own head for the day and would have to hurry, or she'd be late for the meeting of the band parents to discuss the parade next month.

Chapter 12

He had taught himself how to wake up in the morning. First of all, he knew to never open his eyes too soon. The trick was to pretend to be asleep and take in his surroundings. A person could learn plenty by listening, smelling, feeling the air.

All the others called him Crybaby. It was just his name, not a judgment. Every morning, Crybaby lay on a gritty sheet of cardboard against a damp stone wall and began to come awake. He listened for the safe sounds and mentally ticked them off his list. On a safe morning, that old woman with the piece of blue and purple blanket tied around her waist would be knitting. He didn't know if you could properly call it knitting, since she had no yarn. But she would sit facing the sun, and her needles would click-clack to her own rhythm. No one ever approached her, and if he was more aware, he might have wondered what she saw in her lap as she click-clacked through the day.

Another safe sound was that dog scratching itself. It seemed that no more than a handful of seconds would pass between the scratching, and sometimes whining, sounds. The dog stayed with its owner, and sometimes they both scratched. When he thought about it, Crybaby marveled at a man who could see to feeding himself *and* a dog. But he didn't often afford himself the luxury of thinking about it.

Another safe sound was the traffic on nearby streets. There was a flow to it as the world made its way to work. He was especially comforted by the sounds of the buses, the whooshing, and sometimes squeaking, noise they made when coming to a stop.

There were plenty of dangerous noises too. Close sirens were dangerous. Loud voices were dangerous. There wasn't much conversation in the alley after dark. And in the morning, Crybaby and most of the others walked out into the world looking for another day's survival. Loud voices didn't belong to them and brought some manner of unwanted attention to the alley. Rain might also be a dangerous sound; it could be hard to overcome something so relentless. And the muffled sounds following a snow, they were dangerous too.

The smells of the alley were an acquired taste. He and the others each had his or her own aura of odors created from a combination of unwashed bodies and various spills and eliminations that couldn't be avoided. Pungent though they could be, they were the safe smells of the alley. And that dog, that dog had its own smells that were different from those of the humans. Some overriding odor of sickness was around that dog, but it was one of the safe smells.

He wasn't sure what was on the other side of the brick wall, but often there was a smell like hot, old oil. Whatever it might have been frying had lost its aromatic identity to the oil. But it was a safe smell.

Dangerous smells included anything flowery and pleasant—the kinds of smells that were meant to mask what he considered the safe ones. And, of course, the smell of the horse ridden by the police officer with the long baton that he poked into people and places where it didn't belong, that was a dangerous smell.

Sounds and smells aside, before opening his eyes, Crybaby always felt the air with his whole body. Although dirt crusted the lines and tiny crevices of the skin of his hands and face, he breathed his surroundings with acuity. He had learned that there were dangers in the world that might not be sensed in the normal ways. And if he wasn't alert to them, he might find himself in a bad situation indeed. Each morning, he used all his sensors to assess his world. If he couldn't judge his world to be safe, he would remain motionless but alert for as long as necessary. When he was sure his world was safe, he would open his eyes.

Like most elements of his day-to-day life, his morning routine differed immensely from that of most people. During his entire day, all his energy was devoted on a primal level to survival. All his efforts were the sum total of what it took to maintain his life. He wasn't at all sure that he even valued his life anymore, but his instincts continued to ensure that he ate enough, kept enough body heat, and fought off attackers, both the seen and the unseen. He gave no thought to the niceties—cleanliness, comfort, pleasure. He ate, slept, and kept warm to the best of his ability. And, of course, he drank.

When he first found himself without a home, it was somewhat frightening. The circumstances that brought him to it made for an apathetic entry into homelessness. But that first night, that was frightening. The daytimes were manageable. Move from place to place, try not to attract attention, keep an eye out for food. But that night! He didn't know where to go and tried to settle into a dark doorway behind a movie theater. But a large, angry woman chased him off with threats that raised the hairs on his neck. It seemed that every doorway, every dark corner of the world, belonged to someone else. He just kept moving on that first night. There was nothing else to do. By morning, he was exhausted, hungry, scared, and beyond anxious. He quickly learned that this was a waste of his precious resources. When he found the alley the next night, the others staying there seemed to shift in place just enough to allow him entry. He'd been back every night since.

He carried everything he owned with him at all times. He couldn't risk having it stolen. He wore most of his clothes on his body. In all seasons, he wore his long wool coat. It was simply easier to wear than to carry. The coat was missing all but one button, but he'd found a long belt from a discarded robe and used it to hold the coat closed when it was cold. Otherwise, he stored the belt in his backpack.

His red backpack had a picture of a dog and a cat walking arm in arm on the front of it and held his other cold weather gear (two hats, three gloves, and a mitten) and any food or liquor he had in reserve (seldom much). And there was a folded, dog-eared piece of cardboard on which someone had written with a black marker. It read "Homeless Hungry anything will help." He'd found it one morning when everyone else had left the alley and thought it worth keeping. The backpack also had all of his personal belongings: a pair of reading glasses with one lens missing, a toothbrush that he couldn't remember using, a photograph that was folded into quarters, a plastic spoon, and three paper straws. Lastly, there was a copy of a newspaper, now several years old, and he couldn't remember why he kept it. He thought it must be important, since he'd had it for so long. He sometimes lamented that he had no weapon in there and hoped he wouldn't be called on to defend himself or his property.

His only other belongings were a faded and torn polyester blanket, a badly discolored mattress pad, and two wool scarves that he wrapped around his shoes at night when it was especially cold. These he kept in a canvas tote bag that he'd found in a trash can. It was only torn through in two places, and the broken handle was tied to the intact one so he could carry it.

It was easier to find food on the streets than he'd thought it might be. There was no end to the remains that people casually tossed into open trash cans on the street. Food items that they disliked, or couldn't finish, provided most of his nutrition. He, of course, needed to be aware of collection schedules, and sometimes the weather kept those people inside and off the streets, and the pickings were slim.

There were places where a person could sometimes get a hot meal, but there was always a cost. They might want you to talk or go to a religious service. Depending on how hungry he got, he was sometimes willing to pay the price.

Drinking was a lot harder. Alcohol was a contributor to his situation, and he knew it. But he still needed what he got from it. Most people didn't share it if they had it. Like many who have nothing to speak of, they hoarded what little they got, and he understood. He was an unaccomplished thief, so it took actual money to get his own. A job was out of the question for so many reasons. In the absence of theft, that meant begging. Sometimes he'd panhandle on the streets, particularly when people were on their way home from work. That seemed to be the best time. It usually got him enough money for all the cheap alcohol he wanted for a while.

After that first night, the apathy returned and settled on him in earnest. He cared for his basic needs and felt no desire to better his conditions. Despite this, inexplicably, he would cry. He'd find himself standing on a street corner, quietly crying. Or sitting on a bench in a park, crying. He wasn't sure what triggered these episodes and didn't try to uncover a cause. It was just what he did. He was Crybaby.

Chapter 13

The doors opened for him as he approached the supermarket, and the cooler air inside felt so wonderful that, for a moment, Henry forgot why he'd come. He took a basket from the stack by the door and headed down an aisle. He usually didn't shop on Saturday and immediately was reminded why. The aisles were crowded with customers and carts; employees were intent on stocking shelves for shoppers who were reaching around them. A harried young mother held her phone to her ear with one hand while she pulled a crying little boy up from the floor with the other. As the boy loudly protested, Henry promised himself that he'd avoid this place on weekends in the future.

He rounded a corner toward the frozen foods and heard a familiar voice. Ducking quickly back a step, he slid a glance down the aisle, and there was Chiffon. Her back was toward him, and she was talking with a short blonde woman by the doors to the frozen vegetable section. *That*, he thought in dismay, *is exactly where I need to go, and wouldn't you know, she's exactly in the way. Who does she think she is, just standing there in the cool air and chatting as if she hasn't a care in the world?* He stood hidden behind a display of bottled salsa and bags of chips, signs screaming "Sale!" above his head. But he didn't notice them. He didn't want to stay there, but he didn't want to see her, or worse, have her see him. He'd have to talk to her. No, he didn't want that.

But the other woman was smiling and nodding as if the conversation was the most interesting thing imaginable. How long could they stand there?

Since Chiffon wasn't facing him, he began to back his way toward the frozen spinach. He pretended to browse through other items along the way. He just wanted to hear enough to tell him when they might move along.

"... two inches too short! Can you imagine?" the blonde was saying. Chiffon nodded her head and said something that sounded to him like "chariot." He moved to the next door and leaned ever so slightly toward them. "Excuse me," a woman to his left said, as she moved him even closer, causing him to catch his breath in panic.

"Ella wants to go to that carnival." The other woman was changing the subject and clearly not ready to walk away.

"I might take Sunny this weekend," Chiffon said.

"Ugh! The weekend will be the worst! All the kids will be out in force then. Are you sure you want to do that?"

"Friday night is really the only time I could do it before they move on. And I don't mind the kids. They make it a little more fun and exciting for Sunny."

"Well," said the blonde woman, "you're a brave soul." They both laughed.

Carnival? Why on earth would she want to go to a carnival? That seemed especially unsavory, if you asked Henry.

"Oh, it's fun to play those tacky games and collect the cheesy prizes. And I like watching the kids scream as the rides whip them around until they're dizzy. The flashing lights, the crazy loud music—I'm a sucker for all of it!"

He closed the freezer door that he suddenly realized he'd been holding open. The glass immediately clouded with condensation, and he slipped back up the aisle the way he'd come. *I'll just have to get my vegetables later,* he thought. *How inconsiderate she can be!*

He left soon afterward, carrying most of what he'd come in to get. And he was so distracted that he forgot to stop at the dry cleaners to pick up the comforter he'd brought in last week.

Chapter 14

Henry left work on Friday feeling, well, excited. *I could do it*, he was thinking. *Imagine her surprise.* He smiled to himself. *She thinks I'm so straight-laced, so stiff. She thinks I don't know how to have fun.* "The carnival?" he'd say when she was surprised to see him. "Of course! I always come to the carnival when it's in town. Who wouldn't enjoy this?" He'd smile benignly and just move away from her, continuing to have fun. She'd be staring after him and speechless; he was sure of it.

The deli was crowded, and he got his usual order and left quickly. On the way home, he drove past the sad house and was surprised to see people outside. There were two cars in the driveway, and an adult and two teenagers were washing them with buckets and hoses. Henry wouldn't have considered the job to be fun, but they seemed to be enjoying themselves, laughing as they worked.

He went home to change his clothes and get ready for the carnival that was set up in the field behind the old movie theater on the edge of town.

He dressed carefully. He wasn't thinking so much about the actual carnival. How could he? He'd never been to one. No—he was really more concerned about the impression he'd make on Chiffon. He wanted to see that shocked expression on her face so badly! He chose his best shoes and put on a fresh, crisp shirt. He didn't want to look too well dressed; he opted for clean chinos, pressed neatly. He added a baseball cap in an attempt to appear casual yet prepared. After all, what if it rained?

Shortly before dusk, he drove to the field. He passed the large furniture store that had recently opened at the edge of the Connecticut town and pulled off the road. Over the trees toward the west, he could see the roof of an apartment building. Highway sounds reminded him that the town had spread out a lot over his lifetime. When Henry was in high school, these were dirt roads, and there were no buildings at all in sight.

The parking area was full by the time he arrived, and he was directed by some young men in shorts and sneakers. They waved orange vinyl flags toward the far end of the lot, off the pavement. It was far from the entrance. He parked in a rut that looked like it would be impossible to navigate if it rained. Henry suddenly realized that he was grumbling to himself as he made his way across the uneven ground to the gate.

At the entrance, he began to notice his fellow carnival-goers. There were quite a few families with small children, and he wondered about the wisdom of bringing them to what appeared to be a loud, disorganized event. No matter—it wasn't his problem, so he wouldn't worry about it. He was just here for a good time, after all.

More than the families, there were teenagers in couples and in groups. So many teenagers! He wasn't happy about that—he just knew they'd be loud and obnoxious and rude. Self-centered, that's what teenagers were. *Where did they all come from? Were they bussed in from neighboring towns? Is this carnival really the best place to be tonight? Don't they have better things to do? Isn't there homework or something?* He was beginning to have his doubts but allowed himself to be swept in with the rest of the crowd.

Once inside, he thought the crush would let up some, but it didn't at first. He was jostled toward the midway and had a panicky moment. *No.* He shook his head. *It's all right. The crowd is dispersing now; there's breathing space.*

Some of the teenagers went straight to a row of booths that housed an array of games. Some of the others—the girls it seemed—ran toward dangerous-looking rides where others were already screaming and laughing. On one of them, small groups were belted into cars that were then whipped rapidly back and forth. *Chiropractors will be busy tomorrow*, he thought. But the kids continued to laugh and scream, and for every one that exited, there was another ready to take a turn.

Henry was beginning to feel warm. Bright lights hung from poles above the carnival, adding to the heat. He thought he'd be left alone if he stayed away from the actual attractions. He remembered that his goal was to impress Chiffon with his fun-loving nature. Right! Time to have fun. Maybe a bite to eat first. Then, who knew what fun was out there!

Large, generic signs offering "Eats!" caught his attention, and he made his way toward the food trucks. In one, he saw huge slabs of fried dough glistening with sugar. The smell of the grease was, well, unappealing, to say the least. What was it—left over from the gold rush days? And the thought of that gritty sugar made his teeth ache. *I'll have a headache if I stay here much longer*, he thought. He moved away, deciding that he wasn't very hungry, after all.

It was so noisy! Squealing teens and shouting children were everywhere. Parents were calling out to momentarily missing kids, competing with hawkers trying to outshout them all. And the music! So loud that his stomach was vibrating to the beat. He was beginning to feel that it was all too much. He began to look for Chiffon, hoping that he'd see her before she saw him. He'd need some time to prepare. He just wanted to get it over with and escape now.

He wasn't sure where to look. Would she go on those rides? He certainly wouldn't! And if he hung around them for too long, he thought he'd be sick. *Why do these parents allow this? Where is their common sense? Ugh!* And the "games" looked beyond silly. Nothing called for any actual skill, just some luck, and he didn't expect that he had any of that. Besides, he wouldn't want a single one of those "prizes" they offered.

Maybe he could get a drink and walk around holding it even if he didn't drink it. Yes—that was a good idea.

He'd look like he was participating if he had a drink in his hand. Congratulating himself for this thought, he walked toward a truck offering "Drinks!" under its enormous sign. It was halfway down the midway on the other side, and he moved in that direction.

Crossing the pavement was trickier than it looked. He got caught up in a throng of people going toward a roller coaster, of all things. He tried to disengage himself from the group, but a teenaged boy ran right into him in an attempt to avoid being caught by a girl with purple hair and a tattoo of a snake running down her leg. The rude boy just shoved into him! He spun around to avoid the girl who was now almost upon him and bumped into a man holding two large Styrofoam cups with straws in them. One of the tops flew off, and the contents of the cup went first up into the air and then down the leg of Henry's trousers. In horror, he stared at it. The man was not only unapologetic, he was angry and telling Henry off.

"... watch where you're going! Not to mention that those things cost $4.50 apiece! Are you going to replace it or what?"

He opened his mouth to indignantly reply but was spun around again by two running girls before he had the chance. As they passed, he heard wild giggling as they fell into and half-carried each other. When he spun, his left foot landed in something sticky and neon orange colored. He splashed it onto his good shoes. He thought he was going to be sick and began to push his way out of the crowd. He heard laughter as he went but didn't care. He had to get out of there *now*.

Before he knew it, he was at the edge of the carnival grounds. The gate where he entered was nowhere in sight. He kicked a wooden barrier aside and hurried into the parking area.

Breathing heavily, he made his way along a row of cars in the field. He was sure it was not the row in which he'd find his car, but the farther away from the carnival he got, the more he could breathe. When he was sure that no one was near, he stopped and sat on a rock wall along the north edge of the parking area. Struggling to slow his heartbeat, he couldn't remember the last time he'd been so shaken. He had no idea where his car was, and worse, when he found it, he didn't want to get into it with his clothes and shoes in their sticky and smelly condition. He'd have to put his shoes in the trunk and drive home in his socks. He wished he could also remove his slacks; maybe he could find something in the trunk to cover the seat before he sat on it. What a terrible, terrible night! He only wanted to be safely at home where he could try to forget that this ever happened. But he was pretty sure that he wouldn't forget for a very long time. He was grateful for only one thing—that he hadn't run into Chiffon.

What a fool I am, he thought. *Sure, I was going to look like Mr. Cool! What made me think this was a good idea?*

He would feel even worse when he learned that Chiffon had taken Sunny to a movie instead of the carnival.

Chapter 15

Damn, Henry thought. *I expected that dinner would be finished by now.* He hated that they wanted him to take over feeding her. He deliberately intended to arrive after dinner was served, just so this wouldn't happen.

As he suspected, the aide saw him in the doorway and immediately stood to give him her chair.

"We've just started," she explained as she headed out the door. "But she doesn't seem very hungry tonight."

He examined the tray with disdain. The food was so unappealing. His stomach rolled with the smells coming from her dinner. That was part of the reason he so disliked feeding her. But it was more than the distasteful smell.

As he put a small amount of potato on the spoon and lifted it toward her mouth, he said, "Okay, Mom. No small talk first tonight. It's all about dinner."

She opened her mouth, and he guided the spoon to her lips. Most of the potato went in, but some dropped from the corner of her mouth. *This* he hated more than the smells. Her tongue reminded him of a bird, for some reason. She used it to search the side of her mouth for what hung there. It made him shiver to see it. Yet he couldn't turn away. People should *not* need this kind of help. Of course, he didn't begrudge her a meal. But he never wanted to see her like this. He never wanted to see *anyone* like this. He couldn't imagine that she'd want this if she understood. Who would?

He reached for the paper napkin and wiped the potato from her face. "Let's try some carrot," he suggested. Everything was pureed smooth, baby-food-like. If he wasn't careful with the carrot, it would dry on the tiny hairs around her mouth and look ridiculous. Worse, he'd be expected to clean it off. He cursed his luck for arriving when he did.

Chapter 16

Crybaby was feeling shaky, and his stomach was hollow. He thought that this was probably a good day to try to find a real meal. He made his way several blocks to the church where there were sometimes people handing out blankets and coats to anyone who wanted them. They usually had food, too, when they did that. He circled the building to the rear entrance. A flight of stairs led down to a door, behind which were some basement rooms. But there was no one around, and the door had a big padlock hanging from it.

He sat at the top of the stairs looking at the padlock and trying to think of another place where there might be food. He wasn't there for long before a woman and her shopping cart joined him. He had seen her in other places, although she never stayed in his alley. One wheel of her cart made a loud squeaking noise on every turn. The space between the noises lengthened as she slowed in her approach.

They didn't look at each other for very long. Both

focused on that door, and Crybaby urgently wished it would open. It didn't.

The woman began to dig around in her cart, and Crybaby grew more nervous. You never know who might attack you or what they might use, he had learned. He would normally just move away, but she and the cart were blocking his path. He stood, hoping she'd see that he wanted to leave.

She stopped what she was doing and stared at him. After a long few seconds, she pointed at the step where he'd been sitting. Crybaby turned slowly and looked at the step. He had no idea why she was pointing to it. He again turned slowly and began to slide sideways, hoping to make it past before she could try anything. She pushed her cart forward a few inches and grunted, still pointing at the cement step.

Prevented from leaving, Crybaby froze. He was afraid of her and couldn't escape. Slowly, he returned to the step and sat back down. Maybe if he just ignored her, she'd go away. Sometimes that worked. He stared toward the door and waited.

The woman continued to make noise as she rummaged through whatever was in her cart. He stiffened when the noises stopped. He was afraid to look toward her again. Her shadow fell over him, and he held his breath, waiting for something bad to happen.

She leaned toward him, holding out her hand. It held something in a dirty paper wrapping. She shoved the thing toward him, grunting again. He didn't know what to do and stayed frozen in place, saying nothing. But she didn't go away, just kept moving the thing closer to him. When he couldn't ignore it—or her—any longer, Crybaby looked up at her face. She nodded once and forced the thing into his hand. He nodded in return and held the thing in his open palm.

The woman stepped away from him and spent a couple of minutes moving the contents of her cart about again. Then she slowly began to walk away, heading toward the park outside the zoo.

Crybaby looked at the thing in his hand. He thought it might be some kind of food. Too agitated to eat, he put it in his backpack to examine later and stood again. When he left, he was sure to walk away from the park.

Chapter 17

Stan stood and stretched beside the desk that served as his makeshift office in a far corner of the kitchen. The surface of the desk was covered with paper, arranged in small piles in a system only Stan could follow. All the piles but one contained bills from various vendors. One was for tax bills from a number of agencies demanding payment. He sighed and ran his hands through his hair. There had to be a way to get through this without involving Carrie.

"Where's the chicken?" Chiffon was looking around the kitchen.

"What chicken?" He frowned.

"The chicken I asked you to take out of the freezer this morning. Remember? Just after I came in, I told you we'd be needing it before the end of the day."

He nodded, remembering only now. "I forgot to take it out. So, we'll be out of chicken. Let me see what we can substitute," he said as he began to rummage through the refrigerator. It wasn't like him to forget something like that. He needed to get his head together and focus on the job. He shook it quickly as if that would help. "We have some veal cutlets and some sliced turkey. Think that will help?"

Chiffon was in good spirits; she shrugged and smiled. "We'll make do—don't we always?"

"We do, don't we?" He couldn't help returning the smile.

"Okay then. I'll go try to be creative with the customers." She left him alone in the kitchen.

His mind wandered back to his financial troubles as he prepared for the late-afternoon rush of business. Although he disliked the idea immensely, maybe it was time to borrow some money. He was confident that they'd recover from this. They just needed some time. He and Chiffon were a good team, and he knew they could succeed with this. More and more, he thought of the deli as their joint venture. The days of going it alone seemed like a distant memory already.

Business had been decent this summer. In fact, it had been better than decent; it had been good. They probably would have been okay if it hadn't been for that construction project. The roadwork had disrupted the flow of traffic on their street, detouring it only a block away. But it might as well have been a mile away. Customers went elsewhere for those few weeks. Not all of them, but many. Out of sight, out of mind, he supposed.

"Is there a reason," Chiffon looked at him quizzically, "that there's barley in the pea soup?"

Stan grabbed a spoon and stirred the pot. She was right, of course. He tossed the spoon in a sink and walked out the back door. *Okay,* he told himself, *get a grip. You don't help yourself when your head isn't in the game.* He took a deep breath and exhaled forcefully. Then he went inside and got back to work.

Later, when they'd locked the door after the last customer, they were cleaning the kitchen and closing for the night. Chiffon asked, "Want to tell me now?"

He looked at her with feigned surprise. "Don't know what you mean," he said in a tone that suggested he knew exactly what she meant.

"Uh huh. You *wanted* to try barley in pea soup. And you *meant* to leave the chicken in the freezer so we'd have to use the veal and turkey, right? Come on, Stan. I know you better than that—your mind has been elsewhere all day. What's up?"

He hung his head for a second and then walked to the desk. "This," he said, trying not to sound angry, "is what's up. This"—he wove a piece of paper in the air—"and all of the other bills here are what's up."

Chiffon was silent as she surveyed the desktop from a distance. "Okay," she finally said. "Okay, let's see what we can do about this. First of all, I think we can drop the pickles that we add with every sandwich. I don't think anyone eats them anyway. And then there's the olive oil—"

Tiredly, Stan shook his head. "I've been through all of that, Chiffon. I've thought through every step of everything we do, looking for small savings that will add up. But you know what? It isn't worth it. All of those things mean so little in terms of dollars. And I don't want to start chipping away at quality. Our customers come here because of the quality. We can't afford to give them reasons to go away." He sat on the edge of the desk and rubbed his eyes. "That construction affected business just enough to push us near the edge. I'm afraid we could be pushed over it any time now. And the last thing I want to do"—he shook his head adamantly—"is have to go home and tell Carrie that I couldn't make it work."

They were both quiet until Chiffon said, "It really cost you to take me on, didn't it?"

"No, Chiffon. This isn't on you. You're a real asset here. I couldn't do this alone. You're part of the team. Some of our customers only come because of you. Think about Henry, for example." He smiled at her, hoping to convince her that her paycheck didn't create his problem.

Shaking her head, she put her hand lightly on his forearm. "Stan, listen to me. If you hadn't taken me on, you'd be able to pay those bills." She nodded toward the desk. "I know, I know," she continued before he could protest. "I know—I earn my paycheck. And I believe you—I believe that we *will* make this work. This is just a little bump in the road, right? So, I have a thought. What if you didn't have to pay me for a couple of weeks? What if I took a vacation?"

"Chiffon, it's really nice of you to offer, but I can't let you do that. I know things aren't all that easy for you either. No. That's not the solution."

"Stan, what's with you? Can't you let a girl have a vacation once in a while?" She nudged him with her elbow. "Seriously, I've worked here about six months now.

Would two weeks of not paying me help with that?" She gestured again toward the desk.

"Of course it would. It isn't an insurmountable problem. There just are no reserves to deal with it."

"Then it's settled! I can afford to take a couple of weeks without pay, and I could use a little time off. Maybe I'll visit Doreen, God help me. It's been a long time, and if I leave it up to her, it might never happen. It's still slow in here in August, even with the road open again. So, I'm pretty sure you can handle it by yourself. And if you have to work hard while I'm gone, you'll remember why you need me." She went back to work, closing the kitchen for the night.

Stan watched her moving around the room and felt the weight lifting from his shoulders as he thought about paying some of those bills. As he thought about *not* having to tell Carrie how bad things were at the moment. As he thought about how grateful he was to Chiffon.

When they were finished and walking through the door toward their homes, he put a hand on her arm and stopped her. "Chiffon," he began, "I don't know how to thank you."

She grinned at him. "No thanks necessary. You've done so much for me, and I could never repay you. This will make me feel like I've at least tried. And I like that feeling! Have a good night, Stan. Give the kids kisses from me." And with that, she was off toward her car with a wave in the air behind her.

Chapter 18

It felt good to have some time off. Chiffon hadn't realized how much she needed it.

She spent some time getting caught up with old friends, meeting three of them for lunch on the first day of her vacation. TJ, Andy, Mona, and Chiffon had been friends since college. They met in the dorm as freshman and hit it off right away. One of their first collaborations was to devise an elaborate schedule for helping each other get back into the building after hours. They worked well together.

Since those early days, they had traveled together and commiserated with each other over countless major and minor traumas. The others had all married along the way, although TJ had divorced in almost record time. It was one of the reasons that Chiffon sometimes felt herself a little separated from the rest of them.

They had all settled within an hour's distance of each other but didn't manage to get together as often as they would have liked. But usually when they gathered, they picked up exactly where they'd left off when they were last together. It had been four months, but they didn't let that get in their way. They were all in good spirits on this beautiful summer day.

"… and then she called the *police*!" finished Andy as they laughed until tears ran down their faces.

"No one," Chiffon managed to choke out, "no one gets into the predicaments that your mother does!"

The laughter continued as they recalled some of Andy's mother's prior escapades. "It is remarkable," TJ added, "that so many of her adventures involve the police."

"Like when she ran over the cop's foot!" Mona and Chiffon exclaimed in tandem.

"Okay." Andy held up her hands in a halting motion. "Okay, moving on to a subject other than my mother …"

"Can we talk about my crazy neighbors now?" TJ had recently moved into a new apartment.

Two hours later, they parted with assurances to each other that they'd do it again soon. Chiffon drove home feeling good about herself. These friends did that for her. They validated her choices without question. She was much harder on herself than they were. She hoped to ride this wave of positivity for a long time.

She turned on some upbeat music and opened the windows when she got home. Then she spent the rest of the afternoon in her garden, weeding and sprucing it up. She promised herself that she'd call her sister Doreen and make a plan to visit her. As soon as she had time. Maybe tomorrow. Yes, she'd do that tomorrow.

Chapter 19

Henry missed Chiffon while she was on vacation. On the first Monday afterward, he greeted her with a smile when he arrived after work. "Was it a good vacation?"

"It was." She smiled, although he thought there was something forced about it. "I took some time off and then visited my sister in Baltimore."

"Didn't the visit count as 'time off'?" he asked.

"Well, if you knew my sister, you wouldn't even ask that question," she snapped. She was no longer smiling.

Not knowing what to say, Henry just nodded and turned toward the menu board. Every time he thought he understood anything about her, he discovered he had been wrong. He really *had* missed her, but he was no longer sure exactly why.

Sheepishly, Chiffon said, "I'm sorry, Henry. You'd have no reason to know it, but my sister and I have a long history of not getting along. I think there have been times when we've both tried to make it better, but it just doesn't happen. We disagree about most everything."

"Oh." The solution seemed obvious to him, and he couldn't help saying it. "Then why do you visit her?" It was none of his business, and he immediately wished he hadn't asked.

Chiffon became a little defensive. "Well, she *is* my sister, after all. Neither of us has any other family—she's all I have."

"Of course. I'm sorry," he murmured, turning again to the board and giving it his full attention.

"No need to apologize. What can I get you? The usual?" She was all business again.

Chapter 20

"Sylvia!" Ray bellowed from the basement. He was the only person in her life who insisted on including the "a" when he spoke to or about her. When they were young, and she was charmed by everything he did, she found it endearing. But now, years of life later, he knew she didn't like it, but that didn't stop him. In fact, he seemed to take pleasure in irritating her.

Sighing, Sylvie left the pot she was scrubbing in the sink and started down the stairs. "What is it?" she asked, trying not to show her irritation or her fatigue.

"Where is my staple gun?" he demanded, staring at her and waiting for not just an answer but the right one.

"I have no idea," she said as she looked around the dim room. "Where have you already looked?"

"Where? Where have I looked? I've *looked* everywhere. So now you can just tell me where you've put it." His hands were on his hips, his foot tapping. She almost laughed; he looked so much like a child having a tantrum.

"Why would you think I know where it is? Why

would you think I moved it from *wherever* you left it? All I can do is help you look." She walked toward the workbench and began to sort through tools and projects in various stages of completion.

Ray stayed where he stood and pivoted in her direction. "If," he intoned, "you'd come home from work at a reasonable time, it wouldn't be so dark, and I'd have some light down here. Then I'd probably be able to see where you put it."

She didn't stop her search but replied, "Ray, I told you—I didn't move it. And I told you I'd be working late tonight, so you shouldn't have been surprised."

"Right. Right, you told me." He was nodding slowly. "You told me that, once again, work would take priority over me, and you'd be home when they were ready to let you go."

"You know it isn't like that. I told you I'd be late, and we can't afford for me to lose my job, so I need to be prepared to do as they ask." She wasn't in danger of losing her job, and maybe she didn't really have to work late. But she needed to remind him that they were dependent on her paycheck.

"Uh huh." Ray continued to nod. "You'd better remind me that you're the one who contributes to our household. I'm the one who's worth nothing." His voice was beginning to rise, and she wished she hadn't baited him. "However, *Sylvia*, I'm smart enough to know that if you had half a brain, you'd be running that place instead of groveling to a bunch of Neanderthals and letting them run our lives."

Sylvie was too tired to have this discussion again. Ray would get angrier, tell her how stupid she was, and finally storm out, his sense of superiority intact. "Here it is," she said as she slid the staple gun across the workbench and headed back upstairs.

It hadn't always been like this. In the beginning, Ray had seemed proud of her. He'd seemed to think that she was worth having, worth holding onto. He'd laughed at his friends, the ones who couldn't hold onto their girlfriends. Sylvie was always willing to do whatever he wanted. He didn't even have to ask sometimes; she'd just do things for him. He seemed to expect it, and that was all right with her. She'd wanted to make him happy, wanted to be needed by him.

Their patterns were established early. Sylvie had wanted to be needed and had gotten her wish. Ray needed her to take care of him—and of herself. Ray had wanted a household that was under his control and catered to his needs. He'd gotten his wish as well.

Chapter 21

It had rained during the night. Crybaby had used his mattress cover to try to keep himself and his belongings dry. But it was not a very effective tool, and everything was wet. Once he was up, the sky looked like it promised a drier day.

He spread his blanket and the mattress cover on the ground and sat back against the wall. If he was lucky, the sun would dry it out. But he couldn't leave the alley without them, so he'd have to wait. He dozed against the wall and woke when a scrawny cat meowed loudly, as if waking him would produce food. It wouldn't. But he rose slowly and gathered his things.

He was vaguely aware of something wrong with his feet but kept walking. It was unfortunate that he'd fallen asleep for so long, because now there'd be little food left on his route. He didn't care much, though. What he really needed was a bottle, not a plate. His hands were shaking so much that he kept dropping the canvas bag. And now his insides felt wrong, jumpy.

He entered the park near the public restrooms and put the bag and his backpack down, needing to rest his feet. He liked the park during the day better than anywhere else. There were as many children here as adults, and he felt safer among children. They avoided him, of course. But they didn't seem angry, as adult sometimes did. Children just let him be, while adults sometimes seemed too interested in him, tried to make him go away.

When he could walk a little better, he'd make his way out to the intersection near the highway entrance and take that cardboard sign out of the backpack. He hoped he'd be on the right corner and get enough to make a trip to the liquor store on his way back to the alley.

Chapter 22

Henry let the door slam behind him as he entered the deli; he noticed that it felt good to slam something. Chiffon looked up, and surprise registered when she saw who had made the noise.

"And before you ask—no, not the usual," he muttered, scanning the menu on the wall.

"Okay," she said. "What can I get you then?"

He continued to stare at the wall and considered. After a long pause, he said, "I guess maybe the usual, after all."

Chiffon nodded deeply, hiding a smile. "Okay," she said. "Some crackers to go with that or just the roll?"

"I guess I'll try some crackers, sure."

"Okay then." She filled the soup container and wrapped a roll with some butter, adding a package of crackers as she bagged everything. She placed the paper bag on the counter and began to touch the register keys. He reached into his pocket and felt—nothing. Hurriedly, he searched his other pockets, although he knew they'd also be empty. He'd left his wallet in his desk. He'd never done that before! What on earth was wrong with him?

"I'm sorry," he stammered, all bravado lost. "I seem to have left my money at work. I … I'll be back in a while … I'm very sorry." He turned toward the door.

"Wait," she called before he left. He stopped and half-turned toward her. "You're a regular customer here; I'm pretty sure we can trust you. Why don't you just bring it the next time you come in?"

"I wouldn't feel right owing you money." His voice was subdued as he turned back to the door.

"I think maybe you could use a break today, huh?" She smiled.

"It has *not* been a good one." He shook his head, trying to will the stress away. But it didn't work.

"I know that feeling well enough," she said. "Do you want to talk about it?"

"Thanks, but I need to get home," he quickly responded.

"Okay. Sure."

He wished he hadn't been so hasty in his reply. He didn't want to seem ungrateful for her gesture. As she turned back to her work, he found himself explaining. "See, my car broke down on the way to work this morning, and I had to have it towed to a garage. Then I was late for work, and, well, everything went downhill from there. So, I need to get out to the bus stop before the last one leaves."

She thought for a second and said, "It's not generally on the menu here, but I get off in a couple of minutes anyway. How about I give you a lift home?"

His eyes opened wide in surprise. "But you don't know where I live!"

"Well, I suppose you'll tell me what I need to know. Have a seat and give me a minute to finish up here, and I'll be right with you."

And so, he waited.

A few minutes later, she came around the counter and opened the door for him, waving him through. They walked together to the small lot behind the building; he hadn't even realized that it was there. She popped a trunk open remotely to store the tote she carried, and his mouth fell open. "Your car is a convertible!" he blurted.

She nodded and proceeded to put the top down. The September weather was warm, and she wanted to enjoy as much of it as she could. "Yes. That's okay, isn't it?"

"Of course," he murmured. "I'm very familiar with them."

"Come on, get in." She started the engine as he carefully opened the door and sat in the seat.

Great, he thought. *There's probably some convertible etiquette that I don't know, and now I'll look foolish. This should give her a wonderful story to tell.*

She seemed to reach toward him, and he flinched. She glanced at him and continued to place her handbag behind the passenger seat. "Where am I going?"

He was momentarily confused and then replied, "I live at 511 Waterman Street, Silverton."

"See? I live right here in town too. This won't even be out of the way." He was looking around the interior of her car, trying not to be obvious. There was a small, sparkly cloth angel swinging from a ribbon attached to the rearview mirror. The dashboard was dusty, and the back seat was full of all kinds of bags, mainly reusable grocery bags from several different stores. There was an umbrella that was closed but had a broken rib sticking up like a broken bone.

The little car had two-toned leather seats. He settled into the black-and-white bucket, carefully placing the soup on the floor between his feet. He felt too big, out of place. The radio came on, and an unfamiliar song was playing loudly.

"Sorry," she murmured as she turned the volume down while backing the car from its parking space.

He was uneasy that he didn't recognize the music and relieved that she lowered the volume. Some spots on the windshield caught his attention, and he forgot about the radio. *How could she possibly see well with a dirty windshield?* He itched to clean it. The little car bucked as she put it into gear, and he was again distracted.

He took a deep breath and felt, again, the anxiety that had followed him most of the day. It was an understandable mistake that he had made, but how would his boss know that? He hated being the one at fault, hated admitting to an error, no matter how minor. Everyone in the office would probably tease him when they heard about it. And they *would* hear—word traveled quickly through Haul of Fame Trucking. He hated being wrong! This was going to be with him for a while. But he really didn't have time to think about that right now—he was riding (much too quickly!) in a convertible.

The breeze began to lift the hairs on his arms as they drove. He felt oddly exposed but also exhilarated. The air was warm and pleasant. At first, he enjoyed the sound of the wind and the traffic; it made him feel like he wasn't expected to talk. She, apparently, didn't share the feeling.

"So, Henry," she called over the noise, "do you want to talk about your day now?"

"Oh no," he shouted a bit louder than was necessary, "I'd rather forget about it." It was true, although unlikely that he'd forget soon.

She nodded. "I can certainly understand that. I've had days like that myself."

He very rarely had days like this but didn't want to follow this line of conversation. He tried to think of something to say, something innocuous and forgettable. "Do you have a cat?" he finally blurted.

"Do I have a cat? No. Why would you ask that?"

"Oh, no reason really. None at all." *What on earth was I thinking?*

"Single woman with a cat … rather cliché, don't you think?" But she was smiling.

"Yes. I guess it is, isn't it?" He thought he had now done what was expected to maintain a conversation, and he could stop talking. And so, he did.

As they picked up speed, he began to worry more. *What if we were to roll over? There's nothing protecting our heads; shouldn't we be wearing helmets? What if someone tossed a burning cigarette from another vehicle, and it landed on me? What if it landed on* her? *She's driving—would that cause her to do something dangerous?* As they rolled to a stop at a traffic light, his anxieties lessened, and he thought, *Huh! I'm riding in a convertible!*

Chiffon began to rummage through the car's console looking for something. She pulled out a couple of bills; he couldn't see the denomination. She waved her left arm, and the bedraggled man standing on the corner approached. He held a sign of some kind, made from a torn piece of dirty cardboard. Alarmed, Henry sat up straighter. He had no idea what to expect and no idea what he should do to prevent an unpleasant encounter. "No …" he began.

"Bless you," said a scratchy voice.

"Good luck to you," she murmured in response.

Incredulous, Henry just stared at her. He couldn't bring himself to even look at the other man as he shuffled back toward his place on the corner. "What was *that*?" he couldn't help himself asking.

"What was *what*?"

"What did you just hand to him?"

"Cash," she said as the light changed and she drove away.

"Why?" He couldn't imagine doing such a thing.

"Because that's what he's standing there hoping will happen. That's what he needs. Didn't you see the sign?"

"Of course I didn't read his sign!" Henry said.

"Well, if you had, you would have known what I was doing." She made it sound so simple.

"Anyone can make a sign. Doesn't mean it's the truth. How can you trust a stranger who probably only wants your money? I've read that some of these panhandlers own homes in nice neighborhoods and are only taking advantage of your kindness. How can you let that happen?"

"I can't control that." She sounded annoyed now. "If he owns a nice home somewhere—which I seriously doubt, by the way—and is taking advantage of people, that's on him. I can only control my own response. And what I saw was a down-and-out guy with scared and hopeless-looking eyes. How could I possibly ignore those eyes when I sit here in my car with heated seats, on my way home from a job that keeps me comfortable, dry, and safe? How can I not try to help? If he takes that money and drinks it away or uses it to pay his cable bill—I can't possibly know that. And I don't really care about it. All I can do is respond to what looks to me to be a human being in crisis. I *should* actually do more …"

He didn't know what to say. Now he felt vaguely guilty and wasn't sure why. Somehow, it seemed that the conversation had become about her, not the apparently homeless man. But he didn't tell her what he was thinking; she seemed irritated enough.

They rode the rest of the way in silence, each wondering how the other survived in this world.

By the time she dropped him at his door, he thought that the day had ended the way it had begun—completely out of control. And he was sure of this when he got inside and realized that he had left his dinner on the floor of her car.

Chapter 23

Over the next several months, they began to warm to each other. Sometimes, when it was quiet at the deli, Chiffon would stay at the counter with him and chat. No drama, just everyday conversation. The weather, local news.

A couple of times, Henry even ate his dinner there. She'd grabbed a cup of coffee, and they'd sat on wobbly chairs at one of the little tables with green Formica tops. He definitely preferred to eat at home, never had liked eating in public. It somehow seemed too personal to share with complete strangers. But they only did this when it was slow and she didn't have work to do, so there weren't a lot of strangers around.

He might not like eating there but was beginning to look forward to these times for the conversation and company. With Chiffon, he never had to worry about carrying his end of the conversation. That woman could talk to *anyone* about *anything.* It sometimes frustrated him when he disagreed with her but couldn't move her from her position. He liked to think that he was open-minded, but sometimes she was just flat-out wrong, and he wished he could get her to see it.

One Monday when business was slow at the deli, they had talked about those kids in his neighborhood. He had tried to explain how he felt harassed by them and powerless to change that. They were noisy, and he was sure that it was deliberate, sure they knew he didn't like it. They were disrespectful, and he knew they laughed at him.

"Don't you remember being a kid?" She laughed. "Weren't you—even a little—out of control?"

"Of course not! Never like they are!" he responded.

"It just sounds like normal kid stuff to me." She was still smiling. "I remember thinking that I wasn't doing it right unless the adults were frowning and shaking their heads. Rebellion is part of growing up, and these kids sound like they've found a good target to rebel against." She lifted her eyes in his direction, and he understood her meaning.

"Well, I don't see what possible good could come from this kind of behavior. They aren't learning how to be adults this way. I don't understand how their parents allow it. It seems completely unacceptable."

"Well, maybe beneath the rude and loud exteriors, they're just a bunch of insecure adolescents. Maybe they're feeling their way through this life the same way I did—trial and error with a hefty dose of embarrassment on a regular basis. It's how some of us grow up."

"I don't think you understand." He was shaking his

head before she'd finished. "These kids are menacing, and nothing good can come of all this. Someone really should get them under control—and soon."

"Oh, Henry, give them a break. They're just a bunch of kids, not the devil's minions."

A customer walked through the door, and Chiffon rose and walked to the counter. Henry was frustrated that she had, again, gotten the last word. And he knew, of course, that she was wrong.

Chapter 24

Karen and Sylvie were multitasking—that is, they were talking their way through the day as they worked. They frequently did this and were oblivious to the comings and goings of others through the room as they did. There was a steady stream of traffic from the warehouse and the garage, sometimes requiring Karen's or Sylvie's attention. They gave the attention but kept the conversation between them going as well.

"There's a second signature on the back. Thanks." Sylvie paused just a beat. "But I think he's happy, don't you?"

"I suppose. Doesn't seem overly joyful to me, but I guess he's happy enough," Karen replied.

"Don't you think it must get lonely, though? I mean, alone in your house every night. Alone having breakfast. Alone when you have a cold. Always alone."

"How do you know he's always alone, Sylvie? Have you been spying?" Karen chuckled at the thought.

"Of course not! I just … well, he never … I just don't

think he has anyone. I think he'd be pretty selective, if you know what I mean. And he's never mentioned anyone."

"Oh, right! Like he talks so much about anything at all! He could have a wife and six kids, and you wouldn't know it. Why are we still talking about Henry, anyway?"

"I'm curious, that's all. He seems to be just fine on his own, you know? I grew up thinking that adults were *supposed to* be part of a couple, a family. It seemed that a single person *must* be looking for someone. But that doesn't seem to be the case with Henry."

Karen thought before responding. "Sylvie, what's going on here? Why are you exploring what life is like for single people? Is everything all right?"

Sylvie realized that she shouldn't have started this conversation now, but it was too late. "Yes, Karen, I'm fine. Just curious, that's all." She focused her attention on the driver who'd just entered from the garage and promised herself that she'd be more careful in the future. She didn't want anyone thinking that there was anything wrong between her and Ray. Or that she had an interest in Henry.

"There are more under that stack of requisitions." Sylvie motioned to a cabinet at the side of the room, and the driver nodded in acknowledgment and went to the cabinet.

"Well, I think there's a lot we don't know about him. And, mind you, I don't need to know any more than I do. Which is little. And that's fine."

"We may want to change the subject, just in case."

Sylvie nodded toward the door from the parking lot as it opened and Henry stepped inside. The conversation came to an abrupt halt.

Even Henry noticed the sudden quiet. He looked around the room and then nervously asked, "What's up?"

They both looked at him and then at each other. "Nothing," they said simultaneously. He shrugged and left the room hastily. They both knew that he wouldn't have been comfortable if he'd known that they were talking about him.

Chapter 25

It had been wet early in the spring, but shortly before Easter, the weather was beautiful. Henry's walk that morning had brought him past the sad house. Lately, he'd thought there was something different there, and this morning he had realized what it was. There was now only ever one car in the driveway when he passed. He wondered what that meant. Was someone working very early hours? Had they sold a car? Had someone moved out of the house? The windows were all dark and offered no hints. Somehow the dark windows seemed like a good, stable thing to him.

Henry and Chiffon had agreed to meet on Saturday morning. Henry pulled into the parking lot a few minutes before ten. She said she'd meet him there and had a surprise. He was not fond of surprises but would humor her this once. He had to admit that he usually enjoyed her company, and if asked, he might surprise himself by saying that they were friends. At least they were until he knew what this "surprise" was.

Her car trailed dust across the lot five minutes later. She brought it to a stop beside his and walked around it to face him. He nodded toward the back of her car. There was a bicycle hanging from a rack; it looked old and scarred from years of use. "It looks like you're planning a bike ride," he said nervously.

"Nope." She smiled. "I'm planning on *you* taking a bike ride."

"But I told you—I don't ride."

"Not exactly. You told me that you never learned to ride. You may be the only person I've ever met who can't ride a bike. I think it's time to change that. I'm going to teach you how."

"Why? I don't want to learn! It's a skill I'll never use again. Why waste time doing it once?"

"Maybe," she agreed. "But maybe you'll like it. Help me lift it off the rack."

He helped her raise the bike into the air and set it on the ground. Its weight was surprising; it was much lighter than he expected. *Can't be very safe,* he thought; *it can't be very sturdy*. He began to protest. "Look—"

"Okay, so here are the basics: you sit on the seat with your feet on the pedals. As long as you keep moving, you can use the handles right here"—she pointed, making sure he was looking—"right here to keep it steady and upright. You just pedal, and it moves forward. Make sense?"

He swallowed. "The physics of it make sense, yes."

"Great! In actuality, it'll take a little practice before it seems natural. But only a little, you'll see." She crouched beside him and began to roll the leg of his trousers up a few times. He instinctively moved away, but she followed. "Stand still. You won't thank me later if your pant leg gets caught up in the chain."

She walked toward the building, wheeling the bike alongside. "Come on. We'll start over here." He was feeling increasingly anxious and tried again to stop what he was sure was a disaster in the making.

"Not everyone is meant to do some things, you know. A lot of people can't swim. Some people won't use computers. And some people don't ride bikes. I think I'm just one of *those* people." But even though he was protesting, he followed her and the bike to the wall where both stopped.

She ignored him, saying, "Stand near the wall." He did, feeling thoroughly unenthusiastic. She brought the bike up close beside him and said, "I'll hold it upright. You swing your leg over and sit on the seat. Put your hand on the wall for balance, and put your feet on the pedals." After a couple of attempts, he was straddling the crossbar and standing on his toes. "Sit on the seat. Don't worry—I'm holding it up. Just sit and use the wall to balance." Feeling like it was all very awkward, he finally managed to get in the position she was describing. *Okay,* he thought, *I'm up here, and this isn't so bad.*

"I have no idea—" he began. But, again, she cut him off before he could get far.

"I know." She smiled. "That's why I'm here. Just sit there for a minute." She must have learned that much about him—no change came quickly or easily. "Feel how the bike moves with you as you shift your weight a little from side to side." As he was not about to do that and she was still the stabilizing factor, she allowed the bike to lean very slightly to one side. His face was instantly panic filled, and she pulled it back upright. "Next time," she explained, "when I let the bike lean a little, use your weight to counter it." As he began to shake his head, she leaned the bike again. Some instinct he never knew he possessed took over, and he shifted his weight. She smiled. "Get it?"

"I get," he hissed, "that I don't like this."

"Well, of course you don't." She laughed. "You haven't actually done anything yet." He was still extremely doubtful, so she gave him a few more seconds to come around. "Try standing upright on the pedals. Bounce on the seat a little. Feel how stable it is when you're upright."

He frowned at her. "Upright is fine. It's the not-being upright that worries me. And I am not about to *bounce* on anything, if you don't mind."

She shrugged. "Okay. Then I guess you must be ready." Again, he felt that panic. She stepped away, releasing her hold on the handlebars. His grip instantly tightened, whitening his knuckles.

"See? You're on a bike, and you're not falling over. I knew you could do it!"

"I'm also not moving a single muscle," he said through gritted teeth, his brow furrowed in concentration.

"Try letting go of the wall and still staying upright," she suggested.

After a few seconds, he lifted his hand from the wall

for a moment before slamming it back to the stucco surface. He grinned before he could stop himself.

She nodded approvingly. "Now pedal your feet just a little as you walk your hand along the wall."

Again, there was a pause before he tried to follow her instruction. With a jerky motion, he wobbled violently and scraped his elbow against the wall. But he didn't fall.

"Try it again."

This time the movement was only slightly smoother, and he scraped his upper arm on the rough wall. "I didn't know that riding a bike would be so rough on my arms."

"That wall isn't doing you any favors." She smiled. "Let's move you away from it." She stepped between him and the wall. "I'll still help you stay up. This time, try pedaling while holding both hands on the grips."

He tried it. And promptly turned the handlebars toward the wall, fell heavily against it, and slid onto his side on the ground. *Wonderful,* he thought. *I can't begin to guess what I've damaged and what I've done to my clothes.* He said nothing as he stood shakily.

"Are you okay?" she asked. He noticed that she didn't really look very concerned.

"Oh, I'm great. Just great. Just *great,*" he muttered as he brushed at the side of his leg.

"Well, good—then get right back on."

He slowly shook his head. He closed his eyes as he saw her open her mouth to speak.

"Oh, come on! You didn't get hurt; I can see that. If you don't get right back on now, you won't ever get back on!"

"Well, that's the first sensible thing you've said today!"

"We're not here to be sensible. We're here to show you how to have fun riding a bike. Now try it again. But this time we'll start you farther from the wall." She walked the bike a few paces away. "Everyone falls when they're learning. No one is born knowing how to do this. That's why they call it learning to ride a bike."

"Fun! Oh, yes, that's right. Can't remember the last time I had so much *fun*." But he followed her.

"Stop being so dramatic, and get on the damn bike."

And he did.

"Good. Now this time when you begin to pedal, you'll turn slightly away from the wall and aim out into the parking lot."

He did. And he wobbled along for twenty feet or so before walking himself to a stop without falling.

She jumped up in the air and clapped her hands. "Woohoo! Henry! You did it! You rode a bike! Look at you, learning new things! And I think you like it!"

He couldn't help but smile. He *was* pleased with himself—and glad the lesson was over. He'd survived it almost unscathed. Not bad!

"Do it again."

His smiled faded.

"You've made your point." He lifted his leg to climb off.

"No." She shook her head emphatically. "I wasn't making a point. I want you to be comfortable enough to actually enjoy doing this thing. You aren't quite there in a couple of car lengths. Just give me a few more minutes, and then you can quit if you want."

He was getting irritated again. She moved closer, preventing him from getting off without pushing her out of the way. "Just a little more," she coaxed. "You're really getting the hang of it. Don't give up yet. Just a little more."

He sighed and scowled at her. But he righted the bike and walked it toward the wall again. She couldn't hear what he was muttering and didn't interrupt him. He could complain if he wanted—but he was riding a bike!

Chapter 26

That little social worker, or whatever she was, turned up at just the right time. Crybaby was feeling the hunger, and her visits usually meant a hot meal. He'd begun to see her a few months ago. She'd come by the alley at dusk a few times, carrying sandwiches and hot coffee. Then he'd met her on the street during the day. She'd remembered him and coaxed him to a nearby hall where meals were being served to a long line of people who also looked to be homeless. You needed a ticket of some kind for a meal, and she gave him one. When he reached the front of the line, he relinquished his ticket for a sticky plastic tray holding a paper bowl of soup and a paper plate with a little mound of mashed potatoes, some gray-green beans, and a cube of something that was probably meat. It was all hot, and he hadn't eaten so much in a long time. When he was finished, he slipped out the door and made his way back to the alley, full and feeling suddenly too tired to do anything but sleep.

The same woman found him on two more occasions,

and he began to think that she might be seeking him out. Her price was conversation. She would sit with him as he ate, and she would talk. He knew that he should cooperate if he wanted the meals to continue. He didn't say much but nodded as enthusiastically as he could and slipped out as soon as he was finished.

One afternoon, she'd seemed excited when she found him. As he ate his meal, she explained that she had found him a place to live. He was confused because he knew where he lived and wasn't looking for a new place. But he continued to eat as she talked. There was a building nearby that rented rooms by the month. She'd had a client who lived in one but who'd had to leave. The rent was paid for the next two months, and the room was empty. She thought it would be the perfect place for him (she called him "Mr. Pratt," but he had no idea why). She put a hand on his arm as he finished eating and asked him to come with her to see it. He didn't see how he could leave without her now, so he agreed.

He moved with a slow shuffle of feet, unable to hide his reluctance. They walked the couple of blocks, and she led him into a dim hallway and up two flights of stairs. From her pocket, she drew a key and opened a door on the third floor. She stepped back and waved him inside. He hesitantly stepped across the threshold and stopped just inside the door. There were two large shopping bags sitting on the small mattress at the side of the room. A door at the back opened to a tiny bathroom. One dirty window looked out over a dumpster, and he could see a rat cruising along the top edge in search of treasure. His competition, it seemed.

He heard a noise in the hall and looked toward the door, feeling fearful. Misreading him, she reassured him that no one would make him leave, handing him the key with a smile. She took several items from the shopping bags and showed him sheets and towels that she'd found funds to buy. She apologized for the colors, adding that the items were all on sale and all that they could afford. She added that he could live here for two months and she would be around to help him try to find more permanent accommodations, see a doctor, get some new clothes from a thrift store. Maybe even find a job. She asked if he'd like that, a job. In his extreme confusion, he nodded numbly. She smiled and left, telling him that she'd see him soon.

When she was gone, he stood rooted to the same spot he'd been in the whole time. This was a whole new, unwanted responsibility, and he wondered how he'd come to this. All these new things in packages on that mattress. A key, of all things! What was he to do about all this? He concluded that all he could do was safeguard the key. He carefully placed it at the bottom of his backpack and left the room, remembering to close the door behind him, and went back to his alley.

Chapter 27

The Friday after the bike lesson, Henry walked into the deli a little earlier than usual. Chiffon was cleaning a table while talking animatedly to the couple sitting at an adjacent one. She nodded toward him and continued to talk as she wiped the table's surface with a sponge. She was dressed in a floral dress, and her hair was somewhat under control beneath a bright blue headband. Her yellow and white pumps coordinated nicely with the dress, and she looked, he thought somewhat distractedly, very nice.

"… has two dogs too. A real family man!" They all laughed when the man at the table finished speaking.

Henry shifted his weight from foot to foot somewhat impatiently at the counter. He was in a hurry tonight; he planned to stop and visit his mother before he went home. He didn't want to waste time waiting here.

Chiffon walked to the counter smiling, taking her time. "Hi, Henry. What it's going to be tonight?" He wasn't sure—was she mocking him? Maybe he was just a little out of sorts, out of his routine today.

"You know what it's going to be," he muttered as he

pulled out his wallet, ready to pay before she even had his food ready.

"Okay, Mr. Grumpy," she sighed. "I'll get that for you right away."

He realized that she was right. He *was* acting a little grumpy. And he knew that he shouldn't take it out on her. But he didn't have time tonight to explain that. "Sorry," he said, "I'm just in a little hurry tonight."

Oddly, she didn't ask why he was in a hurry. She was usually full of questions, but not tonight.

"You look happy tonight," he couldn't help but say.

"Am I? Am I happy? Hmm. I guess I *am* in a good mood. But I get all dressed up for a date, and the best you can do is that I look *happy*, huh? I'm meeting a friend of Lenny's"—she nodded toward the couple at the table—"for a drink after work."

He knew that she dated and was aware that she was not dating anyone in particular. He knew this from overhearing her conversations with other people when he visited the deli. It was not a conversation that he had actually had with her and might well be too much information. "Oh. That's nice for you, I guess." He was really more interested in his own evening than in hers.

Lenny apparently misunderstood his lack of interest. "Not jealous, are you?" he called over.

Henry felt his face coloring and didn't know why. He most certainly was not jealous, but now the attention in the room was on him, and he didn't like that. "Of course not. Now I'm really late," he muttered as he rushed out the door and to his car. He had planned to ask Chiffon if he could borrow that bike over the weekend, and now he had lost his chance.

Chapter 28

As he signed the visitor's log in the lobby, Henry was aware of noisy activity in the large parlor to his left. A poster on the door reminded him that today was the annual holiday bazaar, a small fundraiser for the activities department. They used the proceeds to buy craft supplies and the like for those residents well and alert enough to participate in the daily activities. He couldn't remember when—or if—his mom had ever been well enough for that in all the time she'd lived here.

The elevator to the third floor was occupied when the doors opened, and Henry hesitated to get in. He didn't really like elevators and especially disliked being in them with other people. But the man in the wheelchair pushed himself a little farther toward the back wall and said, "Well, come on then. No sense spending any more time in this box than I have to, so let's go." Because he was accustomed to complying with instructions, Henry stepped inside and turned to face the doors. He didn't exhale until the doors opened onto the third floor.

Approaching his mother's room, he heard a television playing loudly. The sound seemed to be coming from her room. Surprised, he glanced inside before entering. The other bed in the room was occupied. *Great,* he thought, *another roommate.* His mom didn't like the noise and refused to have a television or even a radio when he offered to bring her either. He leaned over her and spoke into her good ear. "Hi, Mom. It's Henry."

She stiffened at the sound of his voice, her attention entirely elsewhere.

"What are you doing over there?" an annoyingly loud and nasal voice demanded.

"I'm just here to visit my mother." His voice trailed off. He wondered why he was explaining himself to this complete stranger.

"Well, do you have to do that here? And now? I need some privacy, you know!" With that, a hand grabbed the curtain that ran through the room between the two beds and yanked it closed. "And keep the noise down, please. I'm not feeling well." Henry heard the bedsprings protest as the other woman tossed herself to the other side of her bed.

Then she proceeded to loudly moan and complain about not getting any attention. "A person could die in here for all they care," was followed by what sounded like something being thrown against a wall. Henry's mother threw her arms up over her face as if in protection.

Her hands trembled when he gently lowered them back to the sheets. "I'll take care of it, Mom. Don't worry," he said. Inwardly, he cringed. Now he'd need to visit with the nursing staff after all, something he'd hoped to avoid. He avoided their offers to meet to discuss patient care, but now he'd have to try to get one of the two women in that room moved—either his mother to a single room or that other woman to anywhere but room 322.

They sent him to a small conference room to wait for whatever staff was available to see him. He explained that he only wanted to talk with someone about the roommate, but they had him captive, and he knew it. He'd have to sit through their agenda now, as well as his own.

"… and she does like joining the Golden Oldies group on Thursdays. They play the music from when most of them were young, and they like to sing along."

"That's nice," he murmured, wondering how much longer he'd have to stay. "It's good for her to get out of her room now and then, I suppose."

"Oh, she gets out regularly," the nurse in the pink top said. "She likes to play cards."

"Play cards?" He was bewildered.

"Yes. Well, she has to be prompted to actually *play* a card, but—"

"But," Henry blurted in exasperation, "she's blind! And she never played cards in her entire life, even when she could see!"

"Well, we don't treat blindness as a disability here." The nurse sniffed. "*Some* people act like it's the end of the world, but people who are actually blind know that there's a lot left to life, even without their vision."

"But …" He didn't know what to say. How could they not see that it was ridiculous to sit her down with a handful of pieces of cardboard and then pretend that she liked what she was doing? This was exactly why he didn't like these meetings. They didn't know her at all, and they treated her like a child. They acted like they knew what was best for her. Okay, maybe they did know what was best for her, but they shouldn't have been acting like she concurred when they didn't even know her. He exhaled in frustration and stood to leave. "I'm sorry," he mumbled as he turned toward the door, "I have another appointment."

As the door closed behind him, he heard pink-top saying, "See? These families have no idea what we do for ..." His head buzzing, he rushed to the exit.

Chapter 29

Monday was unseasonably hot for a Connecticut spring. When Henry walked out of his office at the end of the day, he was surprised by it; he had forgotten how hot it had been, even early in the morning. It was as if he was walking into a cloud of humid, soupy air. It would be good to get home and get out of his work clothes. The only stop he'd make would be to get his dinner at the deli.

As luck would have it, the window air conditioner that was counted on to cool the front of the store, as well as the kitchen, had stopped working. Perhaps the weather today had overtaxed it, or perhaps it was just old and ready to fail. In any case, it had stopped, and the room was hot. Someone had put a tall oscillating fan in one corner, but all it did was stir the hot air around.

Chiffon looked about as wilted as a person could be. Her hair stuck to her face and neck in wet tendrils. Her freckled arms had a sheen to them, and her clothes looked damp. Her attitude was damp as well.

"What happened?" Henry asked when she turned to him.

"Isn't it obvious?" she responded. "The A/C quit. It's been like this all day." As if to demonstrate, she tried to blow a hair from across her face, but it just stuck to her skin. She looked miserable.

"Oh, yeah." He looked around the room. "I meant with your date."

"My date. My date was … fine. It was fine." She thought for a moment before adding, "No. You know what? It was awful. My date was awful. I don't know why I let myself look forward to blind dates. They're always awful!" She seemed relieved to have said it aloud.

"Oh. I'm … I'm sorry. I wouldn't have asked if I'd known you didn't have fun."

"Fun? In reality, blind dates are never fun. They're stressful. Haven't you ever been talked into it? You spend all this time trying to impress someone else, and then you realize that you don't even like them. So, why are you trying to impress them? you wonder. But you can't seem to get out of that mode, so you keep trying to show them the best you. Except that the best you would never try to impress someone you don't even like."

Henry felt like he was out of his element with this topic of conversation. He put his hands into his pockets and then brought them back out and clasped them behind his back. He cleared his throat to buy himself a few more seconds. He wasn't sure how he was supposed to respond. "No. I've never had a blind date," was all he could think to say.

She grabbed a few bottles of water from the cooler and sat heavily at a table, waving her hand to the chair across from her. He sat and accepted the bottle she offered wordlessly. They both took long drinks and stared out the window. There were no other customers, and he began to worry that she might expect him to sit there for a long time.

"Well, then," she offered, "let me give you a little insight. First, you dress nicely to try to make a good appearance." He remembered the flowered dress and nodded. "Then, you go to a predetermined location to meet the possible love of your life. Don't look so alarmed, Henry; you have to approach these things with a positive attitude."

He shrugged, not knowing if this was true or not.

"Once you've identified each other," she continued, "you play twenty-five questions for a while. What do you do? Where do you live? How do you know whoever-it-is-we-have-in-common? What do you do for fun? The list goes on." She took a drink from the water bottle and nodded while swallowing. "You can't really take too much time to process the answers because you need to be ready to answer your own questions. And at some point, you start to really hear the answers. And now you realize that you're sitting at a table talking to a man whose favorite pastime is making prank calls to drugstores or picking ticks off his dog. Suddenly, you want to get out of there so badly you can hardly contain yourself. At the same time, you realize that you've just disclosed that you had head lice in the third grade. You realize that you've done this when you see him leaning forward slightly and examining your scalp in what he thinks is a surreptitious manner."

"Okay! I get it," Henry laughed and stopped her from going on. "You're right. That sounds like it could be a real nightmare." More seriously, he asked, "Don't you worry about going out alone with complete strangers, though?"

"Why?" she responded.

"Well, it could be dangerous, couldn't it?"

"Dangerous because I don't know them? I guess so, but I've never looked at it that way. Until now, at least." She smirked at him. "Do we ever really know each other, though? I mean *really* know each other?"

"You make a good point, I suppose," he said, but he was unconvinced.

"The truth is," she finally resumed, "it really is *never* fun. I think I only do it to please whoever thought this particular setup would be a good idea. I try to psych myself up to expect good things. But they never come."

He considered what she had said. He thought she was right—it didn't sound like fun at all. He told her as much.

"Your friends," she explained, "or at least *my* friends, seem to think that I need to be with someone else to be happy."

"But what do *you* think?" he asked. "Do you need to be with someone else?"

She stared at him for long seconds before answering. "No," she said, shaking her head. "No, but maybe that's the wrong question. Do I *want* someone else in my life, or do I *need* someone else? I don't think I need someone else. But *want*? Maybe." She sighed. "What about you? Do you want someone else in your life?"

He didn't need to think about it at all. "No," he answered, "I don't want that at all."

"You seem awfully sure of that." She smiled. "How can you be so sure?"

"I like my own routines too much," he answered.

"Too much to allow for someone else's routines?"

"Yes. I don't need or want that."

She studied him for so long that he looked away, afraid he had somehow offended her. "You are an unusual person, Henry," she finally said. "Most of us want the company of another."

"It isn't that I don't enjoy other people," he began. She raised her eyebrows but said nothing. "Okay, you're right. I don't always like being with new people, but I enjoy the small circle of friends that I have. I just don't need or want any of them involved in every detail of my life. I've worked out my path, and I don't need help following it."

She nodded. "It's different for me. I would *like* to have someone who is that important to me, but I know I can't ever give what I would need to give in order to get that. I can barely manage to take care of myself; there's no energy left to give to someone else. I know this about myself, and I don't expect a fairy tale. But my friends think I'm being hard on myself, and they think I'm a great catch for someone, so they keep trying. And I don't want to let them down, so I go along with it. It's really quite tiring." Her voice drifted off.

They sat at the table drinking water and listening to

the whir of the fan in the corner. Finally, Chiffon stood. "Well, neither of us will get home tonight if we keep this up. What'll it be? The usual?"

"Yes, I think I'll have the usual." He grinned.

"You got it," she called as she entered the kitchen.

When she returned with his paper bag, he said, "I almost forgot—do you think I could borrow that bike of yours this weekend?"

"Sure, Henry. I'll bring it with me on Friday."

Chapter 30

The pressure had been building behind her eyes all day. The abundant food smells were wearing her down. Chiffon was struggling to focus on the conversations she was having and was hoping she'd make it through the rest of the workday. She needed to get home and be left alone.

She took customer orders and handed them filled paper bags with one eye on the clock. Someone handed her an empty salt shaker and stood waiting. With a sigh, she turned toward the kitchen to fill it.

Screwing the top on the salt shaker, she came back out front. As she handed it to the waiting customer, a voice called out, "Honey, could you come over here for a minute, please?"

Oh please, Chiffon thought, *please not today.* She located him by a window in the front and walked toward him. "What is it today, Cal?"

"Well, honey, don't take it out on me. I'm just the customer here, and I think Stan's reached the bottom of the soup pot. This was all broth and noodles, not a piece of chicken to be found. Now I know it gets busy back there, but I think one of you needs to be watching that customers get what they pay for." He sat back with a self-satisfied grin.

Without a word, Chiffon went to the register and opened it. She counted out exactly what his bill had been and brought it back to his table. "You know, I think you misheard your *friends*. I think they call you Big Cad, because that's what you are. You're a freeloader who takes advantage of well-meaning people just because you can. But you know what? You can't do that here anymore. We don't need your business, especially since you never actually *pay* for any of it. I'd appreciate it if you eat elsewhere in the future, *honey*."

Chiffon realized then that the whole room had gone quiet. She looked toward the kitchen and saw Stan standing in the doorway, frowning.

Grabbing her things from under the counter, she quietly said, "I'm sorry, Stan. I'm really sorry. But this was *not* the day for him to pull that. I really don't feel well, and I need to leave. I'm really sorry."

As the door closed behind Chiffon, Cal stood to leave, grabbing the money from the table. Neither he nor Stan said a word. As the door closed a second time, someone clapped. Henry stood nearby, looking as if he might leave as well, until Stan called over, "Henry! What's it going to be today?"

Chapter 31

"Ray? Ray!" Sylvie called as she walked through the kitchen. "Ray, I need you to move your car."

Once a year, the employees of Haul of Fame trucking had a baseball night. They brought their families to a minor league game on a Saturday night near the Fourth of July. That way, they saw a game and then enjoyed the fireworks afterward together. It was always a fun night, even the time it rained. Although he was always invited, Sylvie could count on Ray's lack of interest and failure to attend. In the beginning, it bothered her that he wouldn't go. But she had learned to participate in much of life alone, and this event was no exception.

And she hoped that tonight she'd spend some time with Henry. She knew he'd go. He really had to go. And she planned to try to arrange adjacent seats for the two of them during the game so they could talk. She thought that if she could talk to him, she'd learn something of what it's like to be independent, self-sufficient. Maybe she'd learn something about how he could be happy even though he was alone. She'd been looking forward to this all week.

"Ray!" she called again, turning toward the living room. He sat in front of the television, obviously within earshot but not responding to her. "Ray! Didn't you hear me? I need you to move your car!"

"Can't," was all he said.

No further explanation seemed forthcoming. Sylvie took a deep breath to calm herself. "Why," she asked quietly, "can't you move it?"

"Something wrong with it."

"What's wrong with it?"

"Don't know."

She waited for more, knowing that there wouldn't be anything offered. Finally, she said, "Come on, Ray. I don't have time for games. What's going on?"

He leaned back in his chair with a heavy sigh. "My car won't start," he said slowly, "so I can't move it."

"Well, you can't leave it blocking *my* car!"

"Where, *Sylvia*, would my broken-down car be if not in my own driveway?"

"Can't you push it out to the road or something? You knew I planned to go out!"

"If you knew *anything* about cars, *Sylvia*, you'd know that isn't a good idea. I don't know what's wrong with it, and I don't want to make it worse."

The glow of the television screen lit his profile a pale blue. And in that profile, she saw the set of his jaw, the self-satisfied smirk on his lips, and she knew she wasn't going anywhere tonight. She also knew that the car would be moved in time for her to go to work on Monday.

Without another word, Sylvie walked up the stairs and closed the bedroom door behind her.

Chapter 32

She hadn't been there on Monday and was still absent on Friday. Stan said she'd called in sick, and Henry wanted to ask more questions, but it was so busy in there that he could hardly place his order, let alone start a conversation. He was really beginning to worry.

He brought his dinner home and set it on the table in the kitchen. He was preoccupied as he went through his evening routine and realized with surprise that he had finished eating. The summer evening promised a couple of hours of daylight more. And he didn't know what to do with himself. Maybe he'd visit his mother. But that prospect didn't make him feel any better. He knew what would, though. He had to be sure Chiffon was all right.

Henry surprised himself again by grabbing his car keys and hurrying out the door. He barely noticed the three boys on bikes just two driveways down on the left as he backed the car onto the street. He drove to her house with purpose.

But when he arrived, his resolve seemed to flag a

little. He would normally never arrive at someone's door unannounced. He didn't do much visiting, in any case, and never as a spontaneous drop-in. Now he felt worried *and* awkward. This was not the right thing to do, but he could not for the life of him think of anything else. If he wanted to sleep at all tonight, Henry had to ring that doorbell.

And ring it again. And then again.

Chiffon's car was in the garage, he could see that. And he was pretty sure there was a light on toward the back of the house. But she didn't answer the door. Now he was really worried. He cupped his hands around his eyes and tried to see into the living room. As his eyes adjusted to peering through the glass, he was startled to see her looking back at him with a frown. He jumped and nearly fell over the porch rail.

She opened the door a couple of inches. He didn't move. Heart pounding, he was paralyzed by the shock of seeing her see him. "You can come in," she said quietly.

"You gave me quite a scare there!" He was tripping over the words and feeling heat in his face.

"Weren't *you* the one looking in *my* window?" she asked disinterestedly as she crossed the room and sat on a chair upholstered in bright yellows and greens.

"Yes, but I thought you were hurt," he began to explain. It didn't sound like much of an explanation, even to his ears.

"Sit down, Henry."

He looked around. He was just beginning to become aware of the room. Every surface was covered with dust and what looked like debris. There were partially full coffee cups in several locations. It smelled terrible, stale and sour. It made him think of the nursing home, unwashed and uncared for. He was trying hard not to appear shocked by it and hoped he was succeeding.

He wanted to comply, but there was no place to actually sit. He gently nudged a pile of some kind of fabrics (clothing? curtains?) aside and made a space for himself on a sofa. And he sat.

When he finally looked over at her, he knew he could no longer conceal the shock. "You look," he began. "You look … tired." What he thought was, *You look like hell.*

"Mm … yes, I *am* tired. Thanks for noticing."

"I don't mean to state the obvious. It's just that I've been worried about you. Are you okay? Do you need anything?" He didn't know what to ask, didn't want to pry. But she looked awful!

"I'll be okay. I always am in the end. Thanks for checking on me, but I'll be fine."

"What do you mean 'will be'? Are you sick? Do you need to see a doctor?"

"Henry, I don't think I have the energy to explain right now. But I really will be fine."

He was perplexed. She clearly didn't want his help but sure looked like she needed some. But probably not anything he could offer. He should leave now, now that he knew she was "okay." He rose from his seat and replaced the pile he had moved. "Okay then, I'll see you when you're back at work, I guess. Sorry I bothered you." He stepped toward the door, eyes down.

She sighed. "Okay, Henry. Sit back down. If you really want to know where I've been and what's been going on, I'll tell you about it. But I don't think you'll understand."

He didn't say a word as he nudged the pile aside once more and sat again on the sofa.

He waited, but she was quiet for a long time. "I don't know where to begin," she finally said, so quietly he hardly heard her. "How do I explain this to someone who has probably never been depressed?" Her eyes lifted now, and he saw that they were raw with pain. It took his breath away. "There are times," she began, "when I am consumed by such terrible depression that I cannot function in my day-to-day life. It's why I work for Stan. He's a distant cousin, but he knows my history, knows that this happens sometimes. And he's a wonderful guy who puts up with it as my boss. Few others would. At least no one else for whom I've ever worked."

Henry nodded slightly to encourage her to continue. In truth, she was right. He had never been depressed, never had anything like this interfere with his normal routine. He surely couldn't imagine living in this house in its present condition.

She took a breath, exhaled slowly. "Okay. Let's try this. Sit back, close your eyes, and just listen for a while, okay? Try to put yourself in the mental place that I'll describe." The instruction, of course, made him very uneasy. But she didn't seem to be in the mood to coddle. She waited until he did as she'd asked. And he finally did.

She spoke slowly. "Imagine that your world has lost its color. Everything is some kind of gray. Lines blur together, nothing is distinct. But you don't care about that. Imagine that sounds are just noise, alike really. A car horn on the street, your coworkers singing happy birthday, a child crying outside the pharmacy, music in an elevator—all the same, just noise. But you don't care about that either. And imagine that you are alone, exhausted, running on empty. You lack the energy to lift your head, walk, talk. You are not frightened, too tired to care. There are no good feelings, nothing good in your life. There are no bad feelings. None. No feelings at all. Nothing. Your world is stark, barren. You are held down by gravity alone, nothing anchoring you. And you are alone, very alone. But you don't care. If the earth held its breath for just a moment, held its breath and withheld gravity, you could float off into the atmosphere. The limitless, black, cold atmosphere. No one would know or care. *You* don't even care. There's nothing to keep you here, nothing. It would be as if you were never here at all. Your leaving would leave no mark, as your presence makes none. You are less than insignificant. You offer nothing to this life. It has nothing for you. You will never feel differently, never *feel* at all, never be other than completely hopeless. No hope, no worth, no emotion. You cannot begin to relate to other people. You can't really see or hear them. You have nothing in common with anyone. And you don't care. *Being* is exhausting. The emptiness is strangling, suffocating your soul. None of it matters. None of it.

"Through it all, your body maintains itself out of habit. You drink water and don't soil yourself out of sheer habit. But there's one more thing. Deep inside is a tiny kernel of something that cannot be extinguished. You are not conscious of it, but it holds you together with fragile threads because it knows that there is a future. It knows that you will survive and come back to the world as you used to know it. And so, when you are in this darkest of places, the spark burns where you cannot see. You cannot feel its warmth, but on some level, you might remember that it once existed. There is no thought of it really, but it is there, and it's the tiniest weight in your favor even when you don't know it. It keeps your feet planted on the ground, and you don't fall off into space. Because it was there for me once, part of me knows that it will always return when I need it most. This is what allows me to say that I'll be all right, because I always am. I have to believe this. I don't choose to go to this place, but I have always come back from it."

She stopped. He opened his eyes slowly, not sure if she was finished. They looked at each other for long moments before he looked away. He didn't know what to say.

"And that," she finally said, "doesn't begin to convey the vast emptiness in your soul, in the fiber of your being."

Somewhere, something was ticking. There were no other sounds. The air was heavy and oppressive. He was beginning to feel claustrophobic in that room. He wanted to open doors and windows, run outside and breathe. And he didn't know what to say. He shifted uncomfortably and cleared his throat. But he still had no words. It wasn't that he understood so much. In fact, he really didn't, couldn't. But he could see how devastated it made her feel, and he had no idea what to say to make her feel better. He supposed that there was nothing he *could* do, could say. He didn't like this helpless feeling. He would normally walk—or run—away from such a thing. But, of course, he couldn't walk out on her, especially since he had forced his way in.

She gave him a tired smile. "You look kind of pitiful yourself," she suggested. "Yet, I don't think you understand at all. Thank you for trying, though."

"You're right," he finally conceded. "I don't get it. I've never felt anything like that. I can't imagine where it comes from, how anyone could get to the place you describe. The best I can do is accept that *you* have been to that place, and I can see how painful it is for you. I want to help, but I can't begin to see how. Can you tell me how? I hate to see you like this."

She chuckled, adding to his confusion. "It should be that simple," she said as she shook her head.

More ticking as they sat separately in the same room. He could feel sweat run down the back of his shirt. It was so warm, so close he wanted to run. He willed himself to stay seated, but it took great effort.

"I'm sorry—I'm not much of a hostess, am I? Can I get you anything?" she asked, sounding like she hoped he'd decline the offer.

"Thank you but no, I'm just fine."

More silence. Should he leave? Could he? He wrestled with what might be the protocol when she softly said, "You're so solid. Things are so easy for you. You know exactly what to expect from life. There's nothing unprepared about you. With the possible exception of what to do with me right now, you always know the way, you know the path. And you know whether you can manage it and what to do if you can't. I've tried to get to *that* place, but it might as well be on another planet."

"Easy? You think life is *easy* for me? Why would you say that? I mean, I guess in some ways it is, but I don't know what you mean I 'know the way.'" The deeper this went, the more baffled he was.

"You know exactly how to react to any situation. Anyone who knows you can even predict your reactions. You're predictable, stable, steady. Reliable. Trustworthy. Were you a Boy Scout?" She smiled a little.

He said nothing, trying to process this. She went on. "You know what to expect from life. You know who you are. You don't try to be anyone else. I wish I knew who I was with that conviction of yours. You don't ever waste your time trying to determine who you are. I'll bet you never give a thought to who other people expect you to be. You just *are*. You are 100 percent who you are supposed to be. You could not fail to be Henry. No explaining to do, no one disappointed in you."

He tried to reconcile this version she described with what he knew of himself, with the stiff, overly cautious man who avoided risk and uncertainty at almost all cost. The man who was laughed at by the kids in his neighborhood, who walked—ran—away from the unknown. The man who didn't take chances. Finally, he said, "I'm not sure we're thinking about the same person here. You're describing what *might* be interpreted as admirable qualities and completely dismissing the tedious, uninteresting, and overwhelmingly boring reality of Henry."

"That," she was quick to say, "is not at all how I see you. You are a rock in the stream of life, solid and timeless. I, on the other hand, am the water, conforming to every stick and rock I encounter. In the end, who am I? Are any of the characters I play for other people even *me*? All I am is a set of reactions to other people. Left alone, I am no one."

Henry again didn't know how to respond, so he said nothing. Chiffon went on, "I try on different versions of me as if they were clothes. There's the playful me, the serious me, the academic me, the save-the-world me, the everyone's-best-friend me, the aloof, distant me. And others. But every me I try to be falls short. I judge them all to be too much, too little, too wrong. I'm always left with my hollow, insignificant self. That's my reality."

"That"—he leaned forward, holding her gaze—"is not at all how I see *you*. You are a lovely"—he just shook his head as she waved vaguely at her hair, right now looking like a nest for birds—"genuine, funny, interesting woman who is open to new experiences and seeks out opportunities to learn and discover. You are compassionate and thoughtful, curious and generous, intelligent and caring. Shall I go on? I could—there's more."

She smiled and shook her head. "Thank you. I was not fishing for compliments, but thank you for seeing me that way. I wish I thought you were right."

"Well, if I went on, you'd also hear that you are stubborn, opinionated, and chronically late. There's more of *this* too. Don't get me started!" He smiled back. "You are a complex and fascinating person, and I am pleased to call you a friend."

"Well, your friend is one hell of a mess! Haven't you ever noticed that? I change like the wind. I don't know who to *be*. It's very unsettling. You, on the other hand, are the same person today that you were yesterday and will be tomorrow. Life doesn't get ahead of you; you take it all one day at a time, and you are perfectly capable of dealing with it when it arrives."

"Less than you think," he said, almost to himself. "Okay. You want an example of my less-than-ideal behavior? I went to the carnival."

She waited for more, but he seemed to think he had said enough, sitting back and nodding to himself.

"Okay. I'm sorry, but you'll have to explain that."

"A few months after you started to work for Stan, there was a carnival in town," he began. "I overheard you talking to a friend in the supermarket. You said that maybe you'd go to the carnival. You said maybe Friday night you'd go with Sunny. So, I—I went. I thought maybe I'd see you, and you'd see me as someone who *does* take risks, someone who would welcome an adventure."

She just stared.

He went on. "Look, this is embarrassing enough. Do you at least see my point? That sometimes I don't know my limitations, I don't know the right path for me. I rarely take the chance to venture outside of my comfort zone, but I am keenly aware that sometimes I wish I could."

"You did that? You actually went to the carnival?" She was smiling a little, engaged in the conversation.

"Yes, I went to the carnival, okay?"

"And what happened? How did it go?"

"It was miserable; it won't happen again."

"So, what happened?" Her mood, at least, seemed to have improved at the prospect of Henry walking around in a sea of teenagers on a Friday night.

"I got filthy and went home early."

"How did you get filthy? Did you go on the rides?" Something occurred to her. "Don't tell me you rode that mechanical bull!"

"I was splashed, shoved, and driven away," was all he'd say, unhappy at the memory.

"Well, I am impressed," she said, "that you went at all. And you really wanted to impress me with your daring?" She smiled a small smile.

"I did, and I failed most miserably."

"No," she said quietly, "you didn't fail. But despite that episode, I still think you're a rock. Maybe that was the exception that proves the rule."

He looked at her, and they both listened to the clock ticking. He inhaled deeply and made a decision. "There's something else," he said, swallowing before he continued, "but I need you to just listen to me for a minute while I explain. I've never told anyone, and I'm not sure I know how."

"Okay," she said warily.

Henry cleared his throat, looked up at the ceiling. "The thing is," he said, "I answer questions with seven words. No more, no less. Seven. All questions. Seven words."

She stared.

"That look on your face is confirmation that I was right not to tell people about this, I guess." He was regretting going this far, but it was too late.

She stared.

"I can see the wheels turning, see you trying to remember me answering a question with something other than seven words. I assure you—it didn't happen."

"But," she stammered, not knowing what more to say. They stared at each other until Henry laughed.

"I didn't know what to expect for a reaction because, as I said, I've never told anyone else. I can see that you don't know what to do with the information. So—I'll try to explain."

"Please do." She smiled. "I am truly baffled!"

"When I was a teenager, I read an article in a magazine. The author claimed to have studied the number of words we use in common human communications. One of the conclusions from this research was that there was an optimum number of words to be used in answering a question. Typically, more words were too many, too much information. Fewer words were too little information. But seven, seven was the right number. So, I began to be aware of the number of words I used to answer a question. Then I began to experiment with using the 'right' number. Before too long, I couldn't prevent myself from using seven, and only seven, words to answer a question."

"But you just used many more than that to explain!"

"Yes. Because you didn't ask me a question. I offered to explain, and you said, 'Please do.'"

"What would you have said if I had phrased it as a question?"

"Depends on what that question would be."

"Okay. Henry, *how* do you manage to answer questions with just seven words?"

"It's much easier than you would expect."

"I wouldn't expect it to be easy at all!"

"Ah. See? You just gave me an opening to talk and explain without restriction because you didn't ask an actual question. It really is easy. It wasn't at first, and I'm sure I sounded stiff and unnatural sometimes. But I don't even think about it anymore. It's just what I do."

"How," she wondered aloud, "could it be that I never noticed this?"

"Do you *ever* count numbers of words?"

"Well, no, I guess I don't. But it seems like I should have begun to notice some kind of pattern in conversation with you."

"No one ever does. I guess it really isn't very noticeable. In the beginning, I think I expected it to give me some kind of conversational edge, but it never did that either. It just became a habit. And, like a lot of habits, I don't question myself for it."

She continued to stare at him. "Now," she said, "I'll always be aware of myself talking to you. Did I ask a question? Am I asking too many questions? Should I count your words?"

"I don't advise you count my words."

"Because it will always be seven?"

"It will if I'm answering a question."

"Do you have to think about hyphenated words or combination words? Is *mentally unbalanced* one word or two? Would it be hyphenated?" She smiled again.

"I have rules for all of that."

"Really, Henry? You? You have rules? I'm so surprised!"

"Okay. Now you're sounding like yourself again." He returned her smile. "The point is we all have our flaws, our weaknesses. We all wish to be different in some ways. And we'd all prefer that the world *not* see all of our warts."

"Henry?"

"Do I need to expose more warts?" He grinned now, relaxed somehow that this was out.

"One more secret. My name isn't really Chiffon."

"Really? *Now* I'm shocked!"

"Go home, Henry. I'm tired, and I have some work to do." She gestured around the room with her hand.

"Would you like some help?"

"No. No, just go home. Thank you for checking on me. I'm fine now. I'll see you soon."

Chapter 33

After Henry left, Chiffon picked up her pen and resumed writing. A doctor had once suggested that when she felt these "moods" shifting about within her, she write about it. So, she often did that. It had turned into something important for her, probably not exactly what the doctor meant but important.

She had named it her Blue Book. When she felt blue (or worse), she'd add to it. She'd write whatever was in her head and bring what she'd written to the basement, where she kept the book. She chose the location deliberately. She wanted it to be somewhere out of sight, but she needed to feel its presence nearby. She always knew that if she felt bad, she had a place to put those feelings.

It grew into a ritual for her whenever something made her feel bad. The newspaper article about the four-year-old killed when his father's gun accidentally discharged in the hands of his sister? She put it in the book. The bill from the roofing company that had given her an estimate and then billed her hundreds of dollars more? In the book. The picture of that awful haircut she'd been talked into by her (former) hair stylist? In the book.

Her book contained all sorts of things that she wanted to forget, and she never, ever reread what she put there. That wasn't its purpose. It wasn't to memorialize these things; it was to capture them and put them in a place where they couldn't hurt her anymore. And, mostly, it seemed to work.

She sat back and sighed. *Why*, she wondered, *is it so easy to see the worth of others but not of myself?* Having a friend like Henry did seem to anchor her somewhere. The reality of his stability meant that such things exist in this life. Perhaps she was meant to stumble through this life in another way. Their lessons, their purposes, might just be that different. Perhaps.

Chapter 34

Dealing with the mechanics was the most difficult part of Henry's job. They invariably resorted to acting like they knew more than he did in order to get what they wanted. If he seemed to understand what they were talking about, they added some complexity that he suspected they made up entirely. In the end, he usually did what they asked, if only to end an uncomfortable interaction. And he suspected they knew that too.

One morning, two of them, Frank and Leo, had been waiting for him when he came in from the garage. "Henry," Frank said, seeming happier to see him than was necessary. "How are you, buddy?"

"I'm fine, Frank. And how are you?" He nodded toward Leo, who never looked happy to see anyone.

"Oh, you know. Same, same. We could use some help, though."

"What can I do for you?"

A lengthy discussion ensued, at the end of which Henry agreed to the purchase of some obscure tool that he was pretty sure would never get used. Sometimes he thought they just came into his office to take a break and have some fun at his expense. He was sure this was one of those times when Frank casually asked, "So, how's Sylvie doing?"

"Why don't you ask her yourself, Frank?" Henry was puzzled by the question.

"Oh, we just thought … well, we thought … you know … you and Sylvie …" His wide smile full of crooked teeth met Henry's frown.

"Come on, Henry. You can't keep a secret like that around here. We all see the way she looks at you. We'd have to be blind and deaf not to notice that she's interested. Just thought you must have picked up on it yourself by now." He continued to flash that huge smile.

Henry *had* begun to notice something about Sylvie's behavior toward him. But he was horrified to think that anyone else noticed it. *Great!* he thought. *This is just great. Now I have to deal with these idiots too.*

Trying not to let them see that he knew, Henry held his frown and looked from one to the other of them. Leo hadn't said a word, but he actually looked like he might smile. Henry finally said, "I don't know what you're talking about. And I don't have time to continue this ridiculous conversation, so let's all get back to what we get paid for." He went into his office, closing the door behind him. He didn't see the elbow nudging and grinning between them as they moved outside.

In his office, Henry sat heavily. He didn't know what to do. He had noticed that Sylvie seemed to be in the parking lot very often at the same time he was. He'd begun to drive past in the morning if he saw her out there. He'd circle the block, giving her more than enough time to get inside.

What have I done? How could I attract the interest of a married woman? What do I do now? This was new territory for Henry. The only reasonable course of action he could think of was to avoid her as much as possible. Unfortunately, everyone in the company knew that Sylvie and Ray didn't have the best of relationships. But Henry didn't think he had ever given the impression that he noticed, or had any opinion about, the situation. It was none of his business. Sylvie's home life had nothing to do with him. She was good at her job. She didn't need his help. He'd just stay away from her so no one could mistake his intentions. Most of all, Sylvie needed to see that he was unavailable to her!

Chapter 35

Just before Christmas, Henry returned Chiffon's bike to her. He had been riding it regularly, despite the cold.

"You could keep it longer, Henry," she offered. "I doubt that I'll use it again before next spring."

"Thank you, but I won't be needing it anymore. I bought myself an early Christmas present. I bought a new bike," he explained shyly. "I don't buy many big items like this, but I was riding yours quite a bit, and, well, it seemed like it was time to have my own."

Chiffon bowed to him and stood with a huge smile. "I am really so glad that you enjoy riding that much!" she exclaimed. "I'm happy to have been a part of it. You *do* remember that I was a part of it, right?"

Now he grinned broadly. "Yeah, Chiffon. You were a *big* part!"

"Just so you remember. Some day when you're winning triathlons or heading a global bike tour, I want my share of the kudos."

"Sorry to disappoint you, but neither of those

possibilities is likely. However"—now it was Henry who bowed—"I am forever grateful that you insisted I learn to ride."

"Well, now, I'm thinking that there must be other things I can force on you for your own good. Cooking? Scuba diving? The list goes on …"

"Let's quit while we're both ahead, okay?"

"Okay, Henry. And merry Christmas!"

"Merry Christmas, Chiffon. I'll see you next week."

He had considered asking for her help in choosing a new bike. But he decided that if he asked her advice, he might feel a little compelled to heed it. And he knew that he'd probably only do this once, so he wanted to do it right, wanted to be happy with his choice.

He had visited a bike shop to begin doing some research and ask questions. He'd spent a long time with the salesman and left with more brochures and verbal assurances than he thought possible. Then he visited a second bike shop. Here he got more (and somewhat conflicting) information and more assurances.

Over the next couple of weeks, Henry talked to a half-dozen different salespeople at a half-dozen bike shops. By the time he was ready to make his decision, he believed that he had gathered every relevant bit of information. He went back to the second shop and bought a bike. And a helmet. And a box full of assorted accessories, manuals, tools, and must-have items that about doubled his cost. But he was prepared for whatever came his way now—at least regarding his new bike.

The early part of that winter was cold but dry. Henry

began to include some bike rides in his morning routine. Some days he would ride instead of walking, changing his perspective on what he saw. The cars parked on the roads, for example, didn't seem to bother him so much when he was on his bike.

And the sad house was different. Some days when he passed it now, he would see no lights in any windows. He thought that maybe the people in that house were getting more sleep. He remembered the day they were washing the cars, and they certainly *seemed* to be happy together.

Other days he'd venture farther from home and explore new territory. He would dress for the weather and walk his bike down the driveway. He'd get on the bike and begin to pedal. This was one of his favorite parts. The first push of his foot met the resistance of the not-yet-yielding bike mechanism. The first moment was powered purely by Henry. After that, he was assisted by the bike as it did what it was supposed to do. But he loved that feeling of being what made it all come together and work. If he didn't get it started, they wouldn't go anywhere, Henry and his bike.

And they did go places. He especially liked the early-morning rides when he didn't have to compete with many vehicles for the roads. He loved banking around corners and cruising through the city as much as he loved the long, winding roads out beyond the suburbs. The bike gave him a freedom that made him feel like he could fly.

The bike shop must have added his name to all kinds of mailing lists because his mailbox began to contain announcements about biking events. There were serious-biker distance and endurance events, there were rides designed to raise money for charities, there were social events for bike-minded people—and they all wanted Henry to join them. But he ignored them all. Henry liked the solitude of his rides as much as anything else. Some day in the spring, though, he'd take Chiffon out for a ride and show her some of what he'd discovered.

Chapter 36

Spring came early and brought bright, melting sunlight. Chiffon closed her eyes against the glare and tried to swallow the lump in her throat. Birthdays didn't usually bother her. In fact, often she forgot them entirely, her own as well as everyone else's. But this year she was feeling anxious about it.

It wasn't that she minded growing older. There were certain freedoms that came with the territory, and she enjoyed them. No, she really believed that age was just a number. What mattered was how she felt. And right now, she felt hollow. She felt as if she had been wasting time. She felt as if she was meant to do something but had no idea what it was. She felt as if she was stuck on a treadmill of drudgery and boredom and purposelessness. She felt as if she was holding her breath, waiting for something.

She tried to shed the cloak of gloom she wore and opened the door to the deli. Stan was sitting on the floor, fixing a table leg. She didn't notice him as she stepped inside, hopping on one foot to wipe some mud from one shoe before entering. When she put her foot down on the floor, she exhaled a long sigh. In no particular hurry, she moved through the room and removed her jacket. Leaning down to put her purse under the counter, she finally saw Stan and was startled. “You could have said something,” she scowled toward the corner where he sat.

Stan rose, wiping the dust from his hands, and said, “I thought about it, but you seemed to be in your own world, so I didn’t. Sorry, didn’t mean to surprise you like that. Everything okay? You seem preoccupied.”

“I’m fine, I just didn’t see you,” was all she offered as she moved through the door into the kitchen.

Chiffon was up to her elbows in chopped lettuce by the time Stan entered the room. She had several more heads before her on the counter and paid no attention to him.

“So, how was your weekend?” he ventured, taking a stack of orders from his desk and shuffling through them. When she didn’t answer, he looked over the top of his glasses and said, “Chiffon? Are you sure you’re okay?”

She looked up quickly, surprised again to see him there. “What? I’m sorry, Stan. I guess I wasn’t listening.”

“I could see that. Is everything really okay? You seem pretty distracted this morning. It’s only Monday morning, not much time for things to have gone very wrong *here* …” The unfinished sentence hung in the air.

“Yes.” She made the word sound heavy. “Everything’s fine. Okay?” She flashed a half-hearted smile and went back to work.

Stan shook his head and went about readying the store

for the day in silence. They had been doing this for long enough that they could function as a team without much conversation. When the early lunch crowd began to file in, they were ready.

The afternoon flowed past uneventfully. At the usual time, Henry appeared at the counter. "Hey, Henry. What's it going to be today?" Chiffon asked.

He didn't answer, adding to her annoyance. She didn't see why he had to read the sign on the wall every time he came in—only to order the same thing every time.

"Henry?" She wasn't feeling patient, and her voice finally began to filter through to him.

"I'm sorry. I'll just have the usual."

She began to get his food without comment. He stood looking out the window in silence and didn't notice when she was again waiting at the counter. "What's with you today?" she asked.

He shook his head as if trying to dislodge something. "I'm sorry, Chiffon. My mind is elsewhere." He pulled his wallet from his pocket and handed her a bill.

When she had counted out his change, she finally really looked at him. She handed it to him, saying, "You look like you had a tough weekend too." She didn't ask for details, not sure she had the energy for someone else's woes. She turned away and went back to work, but he still stood at the counter. Finally, she asked, "Is there something else, Henry?"

"I wondered … could we talk a little?" he asked, looking around the otherwise empty room.

He was never the one to initiate their conversations,

and that was noteworthy to Chiffon. But she was tired and not sure she had anything to offer. There seemed no way out, though. "Sure. I guess we can talk for a couple of minutes. Tell me what's on your mind."

He smiled his gratitude and nodded. "Well," he began, "you're right. I had a tough weekend. It's just that, well, I'm not sure why it was so tough. I mean, yes, something happened. But, well, once it was over, it should have been *over*, you know? I can't seem to shake this feeling, though, and that doesn't usually happen to me. Well, the thing that happened doesn't usually happen to me either, so there's that—"

"Whoa." She held up her hands. "Whoa, let's start at the beginning. Tell me about the thing that happened to you."

He nodded, looking up at the ceiling as he composed his thoughts. "Okay. Well. Yesterday I went to the market early to get what I needed for the week. Everything was fine. I got everything I needed and was leaving the store. That's when it happened. I walked out the inside door and was in the area where they keep the shopping carts. You know where I mean?" She nodded her encouragement, and he continued. "And that's when it happened. The doors—they all locked. I was stuck where the shopping carts are, between the inside doors and the outside doors, and nothing would open."

He looked at her as if that explained everything. She waited for a moment, but he didn't continue. Finally, she prompted him, "And then …"

"Well, that's what happened. Don't you see?"

"I see," she said reasonably, "that there was a little mishap with the supermarket doors and that you got temporarily caught in the process."

Eyes wide, he shook his head vigorously. "No!" he said. "No! This was *not* a 'little' mishap! It was awful! It was *terrible.* I was stuck between glass doors with people looking at me wondering what I was doing there. They kept trying to open both sets of doors and asking *me* what was going on! I kept telling them, 'I don't know what's going on here,' but as soon as they walked away, someone else would come to the door and try to open it. Both sides. People trying to leave, like me, and others trying to get in. But they had other doors to use. I was the only one *stuck* in there." He took a breath and slowed down a bit.

"All kinds of people had suggestions. Customers, employees, kids shopping with their parents. Nothing worked. Then I heard emergency sirens getting closer. The police officers had the same suggestions, and still nothing worked. I didn't know what to do with myself, and I started counting things. I counted the shopping carts and then the number of wheels on the ground to make sure there were the right number. And those advertising newspapers that they stack in the doorway? I counted them. And the hand baskets? They were inside the store, but I could see them, so I counted them. And the ceiling tiles—"

"Henry. Henry!" Chiffon finally broke through. "I get it. You were stressed about it, and it seems that you still are. I understand why you'd want to talk about it."

"No."

"No?"

"That isn't why I wanted to talk."

"Well, enlighten me!"

He smiled, looking pleased with himself now. "While everyone was running around trying to open the doors, a little girl came to the glass and talked to me. She said that, for her homework, she was supposed to pretend she was interviewing a famous person and write about the interview. She asked if she could interview me, since I was now clearly a famous person. My first inclination was to ignore her and go to the other side of the space. But I thought, *What would Chiffon say? What would she do about this?* So, I told the kid okay, she could interview me. I warned her that I probably didn't fit her teacher's definition of famous but that I'd do it."

His smile was wider now as he waited for Chiffon's pleased reaction. Despite her mood, she couldn't help but smile. "That's very impressive, Henry! I can't say that I really know what I would have done in your place, but I'm flattered that you thought of me as a standard you aspired to meet."

"Well, I don't know if I'd go *that* far, but I did think about how you'd probably do something very different from what I would tend to do. It was actually kind of fun, you know? The couple of minutes with the little girl, I mean. Her mom helped her think of questions and write down some of the answers. But I could tell it was the little girl's idea in the first place."

"So, what kinds of questions did she ask you?"

"She asked about being between the doors."

"Go on," Chiffon prompted when he stopped.

"She asked if I knew how it happened and if I was scared and what I had been doing at the store. I told her, 'I have no idea how it happened,' and, 'I'm not scared yet, but we'll see,' and, 'I was shopping just like everyone else.'"

Chiffon laughed. "Imagine that! She might turn you into a celebrity. Pretty soon you won't have time for the rest of us; you'll be appearing at all the elementary schools."

For a moment, his smile faded. But then he realized that she was joking, and he relaxed. "Anyway, that's what I wanted to tell you about."

"So, how did you get out? Did they have to break the glass?"

"No! They didn't have to do that." He looked relieved as he recalled it.

"But what did they do?"

"The firemen pried the inside doors open."

"That's good. I was afraid you were going to tell me that the firemen with axes broke through and carried you out on their shoulders!" This time, he knew right away that she was joking.

"Seriously, though," he said, "I was concerned when I saw the firemen in all their gear. I would have been scared if they were carrying axes too! The whole incident was alarming, and I had real trouble getting to sleep last night."

"But, all's well that ends well, right?"

"Right. So how was *your* weekend, Chiffon?"

"Oh, it was fine. Nothing so exciting as that." She shrugged and turned toward the door as another customer entered. She offered Henry one final smile as he made his way out. Something in her mood had shifted, and it felt a little lighter now.

Human interaction, she mused, *is such a curious thing. You never can tell who will affect you or what impact you will have on another person. The smallest things can mean so much.*

Chapter 37

Carrie stood holding the door open, waiting for Carson to get into his sneakers. He finally ran toward her, big grin on his face. "This is going to be great!" he said to her as he left the house. "I love playing basketball with these guys!"

"I know you do." She smiled in return.

"How long can I stay?"

"We'll see. When it's time to leave, I'll let you know."

"Okay," he responded agreeably.

They walked to the playground, Carrie at a leisurely pace, Carson bouncing along in anticipation of being allowed to play basketball with the "big kids." His friend Luke had an older brother, and sometimes he let them into the game. This was one of those days.

When they arrived, several boys were already playing, and Carson ran toward them happily. Carrie found a seat on a nearby bench and sat facing the court they were using. Her mind was on groceries, dinner, laundry, and yardwork. She smiled to herself. Some days, a list of chores like that would really irritate her. But she reveled in the normalcy of it all. Her life was good.

With one eye on Carson, she inspected the playground. It really was a nice facility, although she wished that there was room for a soccer field. It would be nice to bring both kids to the same place at the same time once in a while.

As she looked around, she noticed a shabbily dressed man on another bench across the playground. He was watching the basketball players too. And he was crying.

She tried not to watch him, feeling like an intruder. But it was concerning that he was watching the boys so intently. He looked like he was mumbling something to himself, but as long as he stayed put on the bench, she wouldn't worry about it too much. But it was a shame, she thought, that he looked so lost and sad.

She turned her attention back to the boys, wondering if she had given Carson enough time to play and if she could get back to her chores. She decided to call him over and head back home. "Carson," she called out and, when he looked, waved him toward her. He hesitated but ran to her, and she could see the question forming on his face as he approached.

"Aw, Mom," he began, "I'm in the middle of an actual game! Can't we stay longer? We just got here!"

Part of her mind was taking in his pleas, but most of it was focused with alarm on the shabby man who was shuffling his way toward them, one arm shakily reaching forward the whole time. And he was saying something, but she couldn't make out what. She moved herself so that she was between Carson and the course the man seemed to be on. He was definitely coming toward them. She made a quick decision and said, "Sure, honey. Go ahead and finish your game."

He didn't even reply and ran back to the court. As he went, she spun toward the rapidly shuffling man as he approached. Her stare would have stopped most people in their tracks, but he was unaware.

"Tommy T!" he said as he got close.

"Look, I don't know what you're looking for, but I'd appreciate it if you stayed away from my son," she said sternly. The stench was so strong that she took a step backward.

"Tommy T!" he repeated, pointing a shaky arm toward the court. "Tommy T!"

The man who had been weeping moments earlier now displayed such joy on his face that she was completely taken aback. Now she was shaking as well, and she choked out, "Look, you really need to leave, or I'm calling the police."

He looked pained now but repeated, "Tommy T!"

"I don't know who Tommy T is, but you need to stay away from Car-, from my son, okay?" She didn't know if he was dangerous, although he didn't seem so.

His eyes were pleading as he said once more, "Tommy T!" He looked longingly toward the boys. Carrie dialed 911, but before she pressed the send button, something made her turn back to the man. "Tommy T?" she mused, more to herself than to the man. "Was that the boy who died in that terrible accident years ago at the county fair?"

His face lit up, and he pointed again toward the boys. "Tommy T!" He nodded.

"Did you know Tommy T?" she asked, overcoming the urge to just run from the smell and the pain in his eyes.

Nodding again, his tears began to flow once more. "Buh, buh, brother," he finally managed.

Understanding dawned for Carrie, and she said, "Oh! My son reminds you of your brother! But that was so long ago!"

"Tommy T!" he said again, watching Carson run with the others.

Dismayed, Carrie didn't know what to do with him. It would be heartless to just walk away with Carson and leave this poor grieving man out here. And he'd be back, that's for sure. He thought he'd found his long-dead brother. Of course he'd be back!

She cleared the number from her phone and dialed another. "Valley Community Health," a voice answered.

"Patrice Hillwood, please," she responded.

A moment later, another voice came on the line. "This is Patrice."

"Hey, Patrice, it's Carrie. Listen, I, uh, I need you to come meet me."

"Sure, Carrie," she said, with curiosity barely disguised in her voice. "How about I swing by on my way home from work, say sixish?"

"No! No. It has to be now." She couldn't stay here with him until six o'clock!

"Carrie, I can't just walk out of work. Is there—"

Before she could finish the thought, Carrie interrupted, "Patrice, this *is* work. I need you now in your professional capacity. You know that playground at Willow and Spring?

Come to the basketball court. There's a situation here, and I know you'll know how to handle it."

"On my way," she replied.

Carrie sat again on the bench, and the man continued to stand where he was, watching the boys. Now Carrie watched him more than she watched the boys. A short time later, although it seemed like hours to her, Patrice approached from the parking lot. Wisely, she'd brought a colleague, and Carrie was so grateful to see them both.

She hugged her friend quickly and told her what she thought was going on. Patrice told her that she recalled that the young boy who died had an older brother, and they'd been together that day. But no one had heard from him in years. The parents had divorced, the father died a couple of years later, and the mother had moved to the West Coast.

"I'm so sorry for him, Patrice," Carrie explained, "but I have to get Carson away from here. Now."

"Of course." Patrice nodded. "Why don't you take Carson and go out on the Willow Street side. We'll take care of this. I will likely need to call the authorities in, and you don't need to be here if that's the case. Just go—take your son home, and I'll catch up with you later."

Carrie marched straight toward her son and briefly explained to him that they had to go home now. He was not happy about it but complied. It took all of her strength not to turn around for one more look, but Carrie kept walking, Carson's hand firmly enclosed in her own. Her own family had to be her first priority, but she worried about that poor man. Maybe she'd talk to Patrice about it later. Maybe there was a way she could help.

Chapter 38

After the call from the nursing home in the early-evening hours, Henry had called work and left a message that he'd be out for a few days and would let them know when he'd be able to return. He didn't explain; it felt wrong to do it that way, to a machine. And then he sat by himself and tried to puzzle out how he was supposed to feel, what he was supposed to do. Odd that, as a grown man, he had no idea what to do next. He puttered around the house for a couple of hours before he got the call from the funeral home. Arrangements had been made years ago, and the nursing home had contacted them directly. They needed Henry to come in and asked him to bring the clothes his mother would be wearing. This was alarming, unexpected. But he agreed to do it and scheduled a time for the next day.

The next morning, he went to the nursing home for what he expected would be his final visit there. He opened his mother's closet and sighed. There was little hanging there, and a whiff of stale air drifted out. He was not at all sure how to do this. Touching each garment in the limited selection, he chose a dress in blues and greens. He knew these to have been her favorite colors at one time, and that seemed as good a basis for choosing as any. He laid the dress out on the bed and turned back to the closet, wondering if she needed anything more.

An aide walked in at that moment and, seeing him, murmured something about being sorry for his loss. As she said it, she was distracted by the condition of the mechanism that raised and lowered the bed, and her head was bent to the side, so she could see under it. If she was sorry, it seemed to have more to do with the equipment than anything else. Henry ignored her.

The aide finished what she was doing, and Henry was still staring into the closet. "Cleaning it out?" she asked, not unkindly.

Henry responded without facing her, "No. This is for the funeral home."

The woman looked at the dress on the bed and said, "Good choice. I don't think I remember her wearing that dress, but it's pretty. They'll need undergarments too," she added.

Undergarments? Henry hadn't considered that, and his discomfort with the idea was evident.

The aide produced a plastic bag from somewhere and said, "How about if I help you?" Not waiting for his response, she opened a drawer and took out some no-longer-quite-white items and put them in the bag. "I don't think I ever saw her wearing jewelry, but some kids brought brooches in last Christmas, and she has one here. How about if we add that to dress her up a little bit?"

Numbed by his complete unfamiliarity and discomfort, Henry finally said, "Thank you very much for your help." She handed him the bag with the underclothes and the brooch, and he turned to leave.

"Wait," she continued. "They'll want shoes too." She reached down to the floor of the closet and brought out the only pair of shoes his mother had owned. Black slip-ons, they looked more like slippers than shoes. But they were all she had, so they'd have to do. Henry added them to the plastic bag and slipped the dress over his arm.

He looked at the woman for the first time and said, "Thank you. Thank you. Do you think she'll need anything more?"

She glanced at the open closet and thought for a second. "No, I don't think so. I think that's everything."

"Okay then. Well, thank you again. I'd better get these things over there now." And he walked out of the room thinking that she was right—he'd be back one more time to clean everything out.

He drove the short distance to the funeral home, having mentally checked one big item off today's list. He faced an even bigger one now. After parking, he slowly approached what looked like the main door. There were no other cars in the lot, and he wondered if he could even get in. But the heavy door swung smoothly toward him when he pulled on the handle. Inside, it was cool and quiet.

Unsure where he should go or who to ask for, Henry

made his way slowly down the wide corridor, trying to make noise so that no one would be surprised by his presence. "Hello?" he called out after clearing his throat. "Hello? Is anyone here?"

A thin man stepped out of some room a couple of doorways down the corridor. "Yes?" he asked with a smile. "Can I help you?"

Henry held up the bag and the dress. "I said I'd drop these things off?" He had no idea if what he was doing was in any way what was expected of him. "Can I give them to you?"

The man was full of energy. He moved and fidgeted while Henry stood still in that corridor. "Huh. Now I'm confused. Who might you be dropping them off for?" Shifting his weight from side to side, he tilted his head quizzically at Henry.

"They're for my mother. She died yesterday," was all he could think to say.

"We only had one come in yesterday," the man said, nodding vigorously. "But she's all set. I've already done her."

Reeling by the man's use of the word *done*, it was Henry's turn to express confusion. "But no one else would have brought clothes. There *is* no one else. I don't understand. How could you have her clothes?"

"Well, I don't know about *that*." The man sniffed. Suddenly he seemed defensive. "I found a bag of clothes sitting right there," he said, pointing, "on that chair. I knew they must be hers, so I used them. And I have to say, she looks good. I did a good job. Would you like to see?"

Feeling like he'd stepped into a bad dream when he stepped in the door, Henry thought he'd better look, or he'd never be sure they were even talking about the same woman. "Yes. Yes, I'd like to see her."

The man led him down a flight of stairs and into a dim room with tables along three of the windowless walls. Only one table supported a casket, but Henry couldn't be sure whether it was the one they'd ordered so long ago. His steps slowed as he crossed the room. The man was now excited to be showing off his work. "Those clothes seemed way too big when I saw them, so I decided she must have lost weight, you know? I used some stuffing to fill in where I needed to, and now they look like they fit her just fine. What do you think?" He waved his arm through the air toward the casket, and Henry was afraid for a second that he'd yell, "Voila!" But he didn't; he just grinned, waiting for an enthusiastic response from Henry.

Despite the events of this morning, despite the surreal cloud surrounding Henry, this—*this*—was when it got strange. He looked in the casket and into the face of his tiny mother. She seemed to be afloat in pillows, dressed in clothes that could have held two women her size. Two large breasts shaped like perfect cones stuck straight up in the air. He couldn't see her arms in the sleeves of that dress. There was a flowery scarf wrapped elaborately around her neck and held in place by a pin fashioned from dozens of small stones. In a disconnected fog, he wondered if that was really necessary—*would the scarf be likely to come undone while she lay there?*

But her face! Her face was the hardest part for him,

the hardest to look at. She wore thick makeup and some bronze-colored shading around her eyes. And bright red lipstick. Bright red lipstick. *Who thought that was a good idea? How could they do this? They didn't even ask!* This looked nothing, nothing, like her! It was like a really bad joke, like someone was trying to dress her as a clown. That's what she looked like, a clown.

Stunned beyond words, Henry stood over the casket, his mouth hanging open. And tears began to slide down his face. No sounds, just tears. The man seemed torn. While apparently proud of his handiwork, he seemed to decide that Henry was just grief-stricken and would later come to recognize what a good job he had done. He patted Henry's shoulder and said, "You take your time, okay? Take all the time you want." And with that, he was gone, leaving Henry in his shock and his grief.

When Henry had collected himself, he left quietly. He was surprised, when he stepped outside, that it was still daytime, still the same ordinary morning. Later, he would call the funeral home and insist that the casket never be opened again. There would be no service, no calling hours. That had been the way she'd wanted it to be, back when she could express such desires. And he always knew that he'd honor her wishes. But he couldn't take a chance on anyone else seeing her that way. He fervently wished that he hadn't seen her that way. But he had other memories, and he'd hold them instead. He knew that this memory was one that he'd never share with anyone.

Chapter 39

Henry hadn't been to the deli for more than a week and felt an odd relief to get back to his routine. "Odd" because while it was comfortable and familiar, characteristics he normally enjoyed, there was also a dull ache of finality about it. It was as if something was forever gone, and, of course, it was. He sighed softly as he pulled the door open.

Even though it was busy in there, Chiffon stuck her head around the corner into the kitchen and said something to Stan before walking toward the door, taking his arm gently as she went. He found himself back outside almost before he knew it had happened. Once outside, she said, "Are you okay, Henry?"

"And why wouldn't I be okay, Chiffon?" But he looked away as he said it, suspecting he wouldn't be able to withhold well.

"Well, I saw an obituary in the paper last week, and I thought it might have been your mother. Was I right? Did you just lose your mother?"

He turned and looked down the street for a long

moment. Without facing her, he answered, "Yes. My mother died last Thursday night." He held himself straight and still, not having said those words, or anything quite like them, to anyone yet. They felt wrong, those words. They felt like they belonged to someone else, someone whose mother had died. But he knew in his heart that they were true words, his words.

Her eyes full, Chiffon reached up and put her arms around him. "I'm so, so sorry, Henry." There was nothing more for her to say. Henry wasn't at all sure how he was supposed to respond. No one had expressed condolences before this, and he hadn't practiced an acceptable response. Awkwardly, he cleared his throat and nodded in her general direction.

"I didn't know … I mean, you've never mentioned your mother, so I just assumed …" Now it was her turn to seem awkward. "Henry, do you want to talk about it? Do you have anyone to talk to? Stan is filling in for me. Do you want to go somewhere, get a cup of coffee maybe?" She could always offer an ear and a shoulder, and maybe he could use them.

"No. Thank you, Chiffon, but I'm okay." He smiled a small smile, and she touched his shoulder.

"Okay. But if you change your mind, you know where to find me, so …" Her voice trailed off, and she returned the small smile.

He was touched by her gesture, but there was no way he could have taken her up on that offer. How could he possibly explain what the past several years had been like for his mother? Or for himself, for that matter? In many ways, she had gone long ago, and he was the one persisting in a relationship with her. She hadn't recognized him in years. They no longer had a single common memory. How do you connect with someone like that? The only bonds between them were genetic, and she failed to know even that anymore.

He had done his best to keep her comfortable, he thought. He hoped he had, at least. He couldn't begin to guess what it took to actually accomplish "comfort" for her. He suspected that she hadn't enjoyed that particular pleasure in a very long time. He hoped he hadn't made it worse by trying to remind her of what she no longer could know, could remember. There was no way to tell.

Their relationship when they were both younger had been a gentle, respectful one. They both seemed intent on protecting each other, treating each other carefully, each believing the other subject to some frailty, some vulnerability. Maybe they were both right, and that's how it should have been between mother and son.

It turned out that she *was* frail, *was* vulnerable to this awful disease that stole her away even as he watched. It left him bewildered and feeling guilty that he hadn't known how to protect her from it. And now, now it was too late to figure it out.

And then there was the nightmare with the funeral home. He could not have begun to explain that to Chiffon or to anyone. Who would even believe it? He replayed the sequence in his head again and was just as bewildered this time as he was all the other times.

Chapter 40

"Really? He was really practicing dancing in the kitchen?" Carrie laughed as she held the door for Chiffon.

"Well, he didn't actually admit it, but he was!" Chiffon said as she stepped inside the hushed, dimly lit room. "It was really kind of cute, you know?" she whispered as they walked to the check-in desk.

"Oh, I know how cute he can be," Carrie whispered back.

Stan had given Carrie this day at the Obtainable Oasis, a new day spa in town. And Chiffon had readily agreed to accompany her when Carrie asked.

The furniture was butter-soft leather in muted pastel colors, soothing and pleasant. They were silent, taking in their surroundings, for the few minutes they waited to be brought into the back. Once inside, they changed into thick, warm robes and were escorted to the sunroom. They settled into padded lounges facing a wall of windows that looked out on a serene pond, rimmed with old, tall trees. The day was bright, and the sun heated the room nicely.

Chiffon stretched her arms up over her head and wriggled her toes. "This," she sighed, "is the way to spend a day."

Carrie leaned her head back and closed her eyes, a smile on her lips. "Yup. Agreed!"

Chiffon sipped at the lemon-infused water she'd been handed upon entering the room. "I could get used to this," she murmured.

Carrie turned her head and slightly opened her eyes in Chiffon's direction. "Probably shouldn't get *too* used to it."

"Well, a girl can dream, right?"

"Not a bad dream, is it?" Carrie smiled and turned her face back to the sun-filled windows.

They enjoyed the warmth of the sun for a few minutes before Chiffon said quietly, "Carrie, I've never properly thanked you for filling in for me while I was, um, sick last month."

Without opening her eyes, Carrie held up a hand and said, "Nope. Go no further, not necessary. I'm happy to help when needed."

"Still," Chiffon replied, "I'm grateful that you're there for Stan when I can't be." Then she laughed. "Listen to me! Thanking *you* for helping your husband when he needs it!"

They both laughed quietly. Chiffon continued to feel the need to talk about it, though. "I've lost so many jobs and ruined so many relationships by 'dropping out' when

I feel the need to. I can't really explain how good it feels to know that you and Stan have my back. So—thanks."

"Think nothing of it. That's what friends do," Carrie said. "Do you want to talk about it?"

Chiffon considered the offer. "No," she said, realizing as she did so that she meant it. "No, I'm good. I just wanted to say thank you."

"Then consider it said. So, did you decide on the facial?"

"Hm. That *does* sound good. Yes, I think so. How about you?" They proceeded to discuss the various services offered and debated the relative merits of each before deciding how each would spend her day.

"Honestly," Carrie sighed, "I'd be perfectly happy to lounge here all day and not have to answer the phone or referee a disagreement or decide what to make for dinner. It's been so busy lately that just sitting still feels positively decadent!"

"You're right. Nothing wrong with sitting quietly with yourself once in a while, is there?"

"Don't get me wrong; I love my family more than anything. But they wear me out sometimes, and this is great for recharging."

"And Stan says you've had some unusual stresses lately. Like that guy at the playground. You must have been scared out of your wits!"

"Yeah," Carrie said, nodding, "yeah, I was. But only briefly. It became pretty clear that the poor man wasn't really a threat. But before I realized that, yeah, I was scared."

"Do you know what happened to him? Do you think you'll see him again?"

"I only know that he's getting some help. My friend Patrice says that it isn't uncommon for a person to suffer from multiple disorders at the same time. The poor guy was stuck in his grief and struggling with mental illness and alcohol addiction. It's a miracle that he survived from day to day, the way he was living." She shook her head sadly. "I can't help but wonder if a person so broken can ever be fixed, you know?" She leaned her head back and sighed.

"I know what you mean," Chiffon said carefully. "I believe that most of us are broken in some ways. Some small and some not so small. But it *is* amazing that one person can bear so much. I don't know about being fixed, but I'm sure it can be better, at least."

"I hope you're right. I hope he can get better. No one should have to suffer like that."

"Agreed," said Chiffon.

"But," Carrie continued, "I can't help feeling that I should have been able to do something more for him. I don't know what, but *something*. I know I'm not qualified as a mental health professional, but I want to help. So many people need it. I made an appointment"—she seemed to be surprising herself by saying so—"to talk with Patrice about ways I might get involved, might be helpful."

"Good for you!" Chiffon smiled. "I, for one, think you have a *lot* to offer. What does Stan think?"

"He's supportive," Carrie said. "He knows that I've

been itching to get involved in something outside of my own family."

"Well, I wish you all the best. The future beneficiaries of your endeavor don't know yet how lucky they are!" Chiffon reached over to squeeze Carrie's hand.

They were quiet then, waiting to be called for their chosen services. When an attendant came for Chiffon a few minutes later, she held a finger to her lips and inclined her head in Carrie's direction. The attendant smiled and nodded in understanding, and they both walked out to the sound of gentle snoring.

Later, Chiffon met Carrie in the tiny café for lunch. The room held four small, round tables, each surrounded by comfortable, upholstered chairs. The doorway filled one wall, and the other three were lined with various potted plants and shrubs. Hanging from the ceiling in each corner of the room was a basket of flowering plants in bright colors. The tables were painted in trompe l'oeil fashion, each suggesting an elaborate table covering. There were urns of citrusy water on each table, and a small laminated menu waited at each setting.

They ordered salads and happily related the details of the pampering each was enjoying.

"… and once a month they have specials for kids. I could bring Sunny for a manicure or a junior facial. I'll bet she'd love it!" Carrie was clearly delighted with the thought. "Imagine what fun that would be!"

Chiffon agreed that it sounded like fun. They continued to talk quietly while they waited for their lunch to arrive. When it did, Chiffon spread her newly manicured fingers wide in the air before carefully picking up her fork. "It would be a shame to ding these beauties so soon."

"Yes, it would. Good thing you're not a typist on her lunch hour, heading back to work."

Chiffon nodded in agreement. "True. But that would never have happened, since I can't type."

"What do you mean you can't type? Everyone can type. How could you get through the day if you couldn't type?"

"I manage. I mean, I can get by with two fingers, four when I'm really in the zone."

"Didn't you learn in school?"

"Nope."

"How did you arrange that? I thought we all had to take typing."

"I didn't. It's funny … my mother wasn't the warm, nurturing type, and she gave me very little advice. But she once told me that I shouldn't learn to type because, if I did, there'd always be some man around who would expect me to do it for him. Sounded like she knew what she was talking about. So, I never learned."

Carrie laughed. "Maybe that *was* good advice. At the time, anyway. Glad we don't have to worry about things like that anymore."

Chiffon looked serious. "Oh, I don't know if we should stop worrying yet. I'm a few years older than you are, so maybe I've seen things a little differently along the way. But I don't think we're out of the woods yet."

"Really? It seems like those issues don't come up

anymore, at least in my life. I hope Sunny never has to deal with that."

"I hope she doesn't either. I hope younger people stop drawing those lines. But I don't think it's happened yet."

"Maybe we're just a little jaded, at our age?" Carrie wondered aloud.

Chiffon chuckled. "And by *we,* I suppose you really mean *me.* No"—she waved off the protest—"no, it's true. I'm a little sensitive on the subject, I admit it. I don't like to be cast into traditional roles, that's all. Do you remember that guy Austin? The one I met when I had jury duty?"

"Oh, right. Whatever happened to him?"

"We went on a couple of dates. It was nothing earthshaking, but we seemed to be getting along okay. Anyway, we were having ice cream after a movie one night, and he told me he thought I'd make a good politician's wife. 'Wife,' I said. 'Wife? Not politician?' And he looked surprised. 'Of course not,' he said. 'That would be really hard, and you'd hate it. But you look good, and you're diplomatic. You think before you speak. So, you'd be a good woman behind the man.' So, this guy who had known me for all of about twenty minutes suddenly knew what would be 'too hard' for me and thought it best that I just stick with something superficial, where I could stand around and 'look good.'"

"Okay," Carrie said. "Okay, so I guess I know what happened to him." They both smiled. "But maybe he meant it as a compliment, Chiffon."

"Oh, I'm sure he expected me to take it that way.

It probably sounded complimentary to him. But not to me. Like I said—I'm a little sensitive on the subject." She looked up at the doorway and smiled again at Carrie. "But it looks like they're ready for our last appointment of the day. Enjoy!" And she walked down the hall with one of the attendants.

Chapter 41

With the approaching summer weekend came an early-season hurricane. Henry scanned the menu board that Friday, the only customer in the store. Brigit was expected to make landfall early on Saturday, and the highest winds and rain should be Saturday into Sunday.

Stan was furiously cleaning in the kitchen, and Chiffon was taking things off the counter and stowing them away underneath. "Closing early?" Henry wondered aloud.

"Like everyone else, Stan thought we should get out of Brigit's path, as much as possible. I'm surprised to see you here, though. Thought you'd be home battening down the hatches." She didn't look up and continued to clear the counter.

"Nothing much left to do, I guess. I've already reinforced the window openings and brought everything from the yard into the garage. I have batteries, lanterns, flashlights, bottled water, and canned food. I brought the mailbox into the garage too. The car's gas tank is full. Everything in the basement is up on shelves or cinderblocks, nothing on the floor. I've rolled up the rugs on the first floor, just in case, and brought them upstairs. The transistor radio is ready. Oh, and I put a few sandbags along the front of the yard to try to direct excess water to the nearest drain. I think I'm all set."

By the time he'd finished, Chiffon was standing, staring at him with an incredulous expression. "You can't be serious! You've really done all of that in anticipation of a storm that we *still* aren't certain will hit us?"

"When we're certain, it'll be too late."

Chiffon couldn't really argue with his logic. "Yes, but I don't know anyone who does all of that in anticipation of a storm!"

"Yes, you do."

"Anyone *else*, I mean."

He shrugged. "It would be irresponsible," he said, "to do less. What preparations have you made then? At home, I mean."

She laughed. "Let's see. I closed all the windows but one. And I made a plan to bring some water bottles home with me tonight. And, um, I guess that's about it." She grinned at him. "Think my plan seems a little lacking, Henry?"

"I don't know how you survive, Chiffon." She laughed, and he frowned and shook his head. "It's troubling that anyone would fail to prepare a little better than that."

She laughed again. "I'm sorry if I'm shockingly irresponsible. Truth is I like storms and hurricanes." She held up her hand to stop his protest. "I know, I know. But I've never had a bad experience like that. I've been very lucky, and I know it. But I like the power and fury of a good storm. And there's nothing better than the air following a storm. I'll admit that I'm disappointed when they pass us by completely."

"You are unbelievable! How can you *like* such a deadly force? Don't you know how dangerous a hurricane can be? Don't you follow the news? This one has already caused a lot of damage on the way up the coast. This isn't some 'good time' to kick off the weekend!"

"Yeah, I know. I'm sorry I don't fit the mold here, but I just don't. So," she glanced into the kitchen at the stove, "we don't have much left, but what can I get you?"

Now it was Henry who stared. She really wasn't at all flustered. In fact, she was smiling again. "I'll have two containers of the usual," was all he could manage.

"Let me check and see if we have two left," she answered, disappearing into the kitchen.

As she filled his soup containers, Chiffon recalled an early hurricane in her life. She was only about five at the time and remembered standing at a window. The window frame was old, with many layers of paint, some of it chipping off. She remembered pressing her hands and face against the window, watching the trees whip wildly in the wind. She could smell the mixture of old paint and somewhat newer dust on the warm wood. She felt safe behind that pane of glass. She felt like it separated her from all that fury. She could be part of it, yet not. She loved that feeling and probably protested loudly when some adult took her hand and led her away from the window.

Back out front, she gave Henry his order and wished him good luck with the storm. She didn't feel like she needed luck herself.

Chapter 42

"Henry." Sylvie stood in the doorway, blocking his exit. "I really need to talk to you. Can we talk for a few minutes?"

Looking caught off guard, Henry was wondering how he'd allowed himself to be trapped like this. He cleared his throat and looked frantically toward the clock for help that wasn't there. "Okay, Sylvie. I have a few minutes." He gestured to a chair and went back behind his desk. He was further panicked when she reached around and closed the door before sitting.

She smiled at him but looked kind of nervous. *Oh God!* he thought. *Here it comes! What am I going to do?*

Sylvie began to talk, but all Henry could do was struggle for a way out. Thoughts whipped through his head at a frantic pace until he heard her say "… next Friday."

In the pause that followed, he started to shake his head saying, "Next Friday? Next Friday, no, not good at all. Next Friday won't work at all."

Sylvie looked at him oddly and waited for him to

continue. She seemed to be at a loss for words and looked confused.

"I'm sorry, Sylvie. I really am, but it would just be impossible."

"But, Henry," she finally said as he continued to shake his head, "I already have a flight reservation and have worked out all the other details. It has to be Friday, I'm afraid."

It was Henry's turn to be baffled. He just stared at her, wrapped in his confusion. He didn't know where to look, what to say. And now he had no idea what they were talking about, only what he *thought* they were going to talk about.

Sylvie took a deep breath. "Maybe," she started again, "I didn't explain that well. Let me try again."

He just nodded.

She looked down into her lap, where her hands lay quietly. Raising her eyes to his, she said, "Henry, I'm sorry to give you such short notice, but I'm leaving my job next Friday, and I'll be leaving the area immediately after that. I'm leaving Ray, although he doesn't know it yet, and I'm moving to Arizona."

Henry stared, trying to process this new information and trying to get out of the fog of the conversation he'd expected to have. "Okay," he said reasonably, "okay, Sylvie. I get it. I think."

Her smile seemed a little more confident. "I know. I know it's unexpected and sudden. I don't think it could ever have been otherwise, though. It's no secret that Ray and I have not been a model, happily married couple. I probably should have done this a long time ago. I do believe that it will be good for both of us. But, in any case, I need to do this now for myself." She shook her head slightly, and he saw wonder on her face. "It's been a long time," she said quietly, "since I've done something big for myself."

"Where will you go exactly? And what will you do?" Henry found that he was curious.

"My sister is in Arizona, and I'll go there. She's already found me a job and an apartment. I owe her a lot; she's made it all possible. I've managed to save some money, and I'll leave half of it for Ray. I expect he'll have a more difficult time than I will. But he'll be okay."

The conversation turned to the practical matters of what to do about her work and how to replace her at the trucking company. As the minutes passed, Henry's anxiety dissipated, and he already wondered how he'd gotten himself into such a state. *The reality of her leaving will be much easier to deal with than my silly expectations have been*, he thought with chagrin.

Sylvie was about to open the door and leave when she stopped and turned back to him. "Henry," she said, "before I leave, I want to thank you for being such an inspiration to me."

Baffled again, Henry just stared.

"I've wanted to talk to you several times through these weeks as I came to this decision. In the end, I know I needed to make the decision on my own. But watching you be so self-confident, so able, gave me hope that I, too, could be a person who took care of herself and needed no one else to do it for her. Thank you for giving me someone to look up to when I needed it most." And she was gone.

Chapter 43

Ray walked into the kitchen from the driveway and frowned. By now, Sylvia should have been home from work and getting dinner ready. But there were no lights on, and there was no smell of food. He tried to remember if she'd said anything about being late but could recall nothing. In fact, he couldn't recall the last time they'd talked at all.

His annoyance growing, he walked through the house. He didn't call out to her, knowing there'd be no answer. She wasn't there.

He went upstairs, just in case. When he stepped into the bedroom, he saw the aftermath of someone packing and leaving quickly. On the bed was an envelope with his name on it. He picked it up and made his way back down to the living room. He grabbed a beer from the kitchen before sitting to read the letter she'd left.

"Dear Ray," he read aloud, then took a swallow of the beer. "By now, you know that I'm gone." *Didn't take a genius,* he thought. "We've both known for a long time that we don't work together. I wish it had turned out differently for us, I really do. Maybe apart we'll find the happiness we couldn't seem to find together. I had some money saved, and I left you half of it. It should be enough, if you're careful, to last you awhile. Hopefully, it'll last long enough for you to figure out what you'll do next. Blah, blah, blah."

He tossed the page on the floor, not bothering to finish reading it. He wasn't angry, he realized. He was surprised. Years ago, he'd thought she should do exactly this. But as time went on, he came to believe that she never would, never could.

Once, on a daytime talk show, he'd seen a story about relationships. Well, he'd actually seen a lot of those on daytime television. But this particular one had a small group of people scattered across a pair of curved sofas with a small table between them. They'd been talking about how, in any relationship, there was always one person who cared more than the other, one who loved more. He remembered thinking that they were all wrong. They'd sat on those sofas whining about how hard it was to "love more." Ray wanted to hear from the other side. Didn't they know how hard it was to spend every day with a martyr? It was so irritating to be around someone who you couldn't make go away because they "cared more." They should have had at least one person on that set who could tell them all how annoying they were. That's what they'd needed.

If he was honest, he knew that she was right. They should have ended this long ago. He blamed her for holding on. He could have let it go at any time, but she hung on.

He stepped over the letter and went back to the kitchen for another beer. As he opened the refrigerator, he wondered if there were any leftovers in there that he could have for dinner.

Chapter 44

"Henry! Wait up!" Chiffon called, and he reluctantly brought his bike to a stop. "My old-fashioned, low-tech equipment can't keep up with yours," she managed as she tried to catch her breath.

He'd thought this route was largely flat and that she wouldn't have any trouble, but he was wrong. She dismounted and walked her bike toward him. They stood for a minute while she recovered. At last she said, "Can we walk for a bit? I want to enjoy being out here, and I can't when it's so much work!"

It was definitely not what he'd had in mind, but he agreed when she smiled encouragingly. He removed his helmet and attached it to the bike, and they began to walk in tandem.

He'd been riding the trails through this state park for months and thought she might like to see some of it. They'd met in the parking lot below and set out in the early afternoon. The sun was warm and pleasant; they hadn't gone far before both removed their jackets. He hadn't realized the distance that had stretched between them, lost in his own thoughts.

The trees along both sides on the path were tall, and the ground around them was shrouded in thick layers of pine straw. Sun streaked through, and they passed in and out of it as they walked. Chiffon bent and picked up a small piece of a pine branch. She held it to him and said, "Smell. What does it remind you of?" He leaned forward, pulling back as she brought it closer. "It won't bite you." She smiled. "Just smell it."

He did and shrugged. "Come on—what does it smell like?" she asked again.

"It smells like a Christmas tree branch."

"It does, doesn't it? That's probably what most people would say." She smiled again. "To me, it smells like the best time of my life. Let's leave the bikes here and walk a little way down this trail." She pointed toward a narrow dirt path.

He didn't like the idea at all, and it showed in his expression. "Look, if it makes you feel better, we can lock the bikes together around this tree." She walked toward a small but sturdy-looking tree. Reluctantly, he followed. "There," she said as she snapped the lock closed. "They'll be here when we get back." He wondered exactly when that would be, but he followed her silently toward the path, thinking about the chores he planned to finish before dinner and worrying that there might not be time for them now.

It was peaceful as they walked, surrounded by the trees and the noises of the woods. Besides the birds and the rustling of small animals in the undergrowth, there were occasional distant animal calls. He began to feel glad that they were walking. He was sure that he'd get drowsy and fall asleep if he stopped and sat.

"The summer I was twelve," she said, interrupting his quiet, "was the best summer of my life. And the best part of that summer was a week I spent with my best friend and her family. They owned an old hunting camp deep in the woods. It was pretty remote; there wasn't much around the area. There was no electricity, no running water. There was an outhouse that someone bigger than we were would periodically clean. The cabin itself was just one big room full of beds. There was an old wood stove and a table with some folding chairs, but the rest of the floor space was covered with various folding beds and cots. The walls were wood panels, and the floor was gray-painted wood. The only foundation was a stack of cinderblocks at each corner of the building, a few more spaced underneath. They kept it more or less level but did nothing to prevent the nests of any number of small animals." Her eyes had a faraway look as she recalled the place.

"I was so excited to be going," she continued. "It had been a good summer at home in the city. It was already August, and soon we'd have to think about going back to school. But first, we'd have this week of camping together. It was a three-hour car ride, about as far as either of us had ever been. Kind of the edge of our known world, you know? Candace and I thought we *were* the world that summer."

She walked a few steps in silence before continuing. "We cooked all of our meals outside that week. Candace's dad arranged a ring of stones and balanced an old grate on the top. He lit a fire under the grate every night. We roasted hotdogs on sticks and made s'mores. Sometimes we'd heat baked beans or stew in a beat up old pot. The fire generated a lot of smoke, and everything—hair, clothing, everything—smelled smoky all week. Have you ever done any camping, Henry?"

He wrinkled his nose slightly and replied, "No, and I've never even been tempted." He wondered why anyone would enjoy such a thing.

"Well," she continued, "it might sound pretty boring, right? I mean, no TV, no telephone, no convenience stores. But Candace and I had the best week ever. There were some huge boulders in the hill leading down from the cabin. The sun was hot on them all morning, but they were shaded in the afternoon. It's hard to believe that we actually found them comfortable, but we'd bring books and climb up on them after lunch. We'd stretch out on the warm stone and read for hours, cooled by the shade and the breeze. By midafternoon, we'd begin to get restless and go for long walks. We'd walk and talk—never ran out of things to talk about—for miles on dirt roads and wooded paths like this one.

"There was a well-packed dirt road that led to a lake, and sometimes we'd go there. The sunlight in the trees made lacy patterns along the road, and we read them like tea leaves." She laughed at the memory. "Vacationers like us weren't the only ones using the lake and its shady grounds. Lots of locals went there too. There were usually several families picnicking and groups of young people swimming and sunning themselves on the shore. We didn't know anyone but loved watching these other kids interact. We'd invent entire lives for them, based on the little that we saw and heard. We'd add a healthy dose of imagination and give them nicknames. Then we'd predict their futures as architects and lawyers, planning all kinds of good lives for them. Hopeful for ourselves but not bold enough to predict such glowing futures of our own.

"On the walk back, our sneakers dusty with the fine, dry dirt of the well-worn road, we'd sing. Not under-your-breath little songs. No, we'd sing at the top of our lungs. Shouting more than singing. Every song we could think of, we'd sing. And then we'd laugh. We'd sing until we'd be laughing so hard we couldn't even stand. Holding on to trees and bent over in laughter until we couldn't breathe. And then we'd think of a new song and start again. Our hands would be sticky with the sap from those trees and filthy from everything else we touched afterward. And they smelled"—she waved the little branch in the air—"just like this. So, whenever I smell pine sap, I remember that week in that summer that was the best ever. I flash back to a couple of girls bobbing along a dirt road without a care in the world, unaware of the future, unconcerned with the past, living in the moment like I never had before or have since." She still smiled at the memories.

"Neither of those girls knew that one of them would soon lose her mother to cancer, or that the other would be blindsided by the suicide of her brother. They weren't thinking about cheating husbands or stolen youth, fender benders or bad-hair days. They were filled with joy, pure joy. The kind that hasn't been tempered by anything truly bad." Somber now, she shook her head slowly.

Henry didn't say anything. He had no idea what he *should* say. He supposed she didn't need him to be anything but witness to her story. They walked the rest of the way back to their bikes in silence. Not tense, just quiet.

Chapter 45

"And I thought *I* was early today. What brings you in at this hour?" Chiffon called into the kitchen as she removed her jacket and stashed her purse under the counter.

Stan came out front with a handful of order tickets, glasses sliding down his nose as he looked over them at Chiffon. "Just trying to get ahead of this," he said, waving the orders toward the kitchen, "before it gets too busy. What about you? What's your excuse?"

"I told the printer that I'd get the new catering menu to them by today, so …" She smiled. "Fun, isn't it?"

Stan took his glasses off and leaned against the doorway. "I think," he said quietly, "we need to talk. Let's go back to the 'office' and sit for a minute."

Chiffon felt the blood rush to her ears and heard the roar it created. "Oh," was all she could say at first. "Oh, okay. Do I need—should I bring anything? Stan, are you letting me go? Am I unemployed again?"

Midway through the kitchen, he stopped and turned,

laughing. "Of course not! Just come sit down for a minute." Shaking his head, he chuckled. "Why would you even think that?"

"I thought that," she said a little defensively, "because, in my experience, when a boss says, 'Let's talk,' it means 'Let's talk about your exit.'" But the roaring in her head had stopped.

"Well, maybe that's true. But one problem with that is that I don't think of either of us as 'the boss.'"

"What are you talking about? This is your place. I work for you." She was still not convinced that she liked the direction this was taking.

"I guess I never told you"—he was smiling at the memory—"about the day you called me to say you'd lost your job and wondered if I was hiring. What you didn't know was that I'd not even thought of hiring. In no way did I think I could afford to hire someone. I wasn't sure that day how long I could guarantee *either* of us employment. I wouldn't have taken on anyone but you, and I thought I was doing you a favor. But turns out that *you* did *me* the favor."

"How did I do you a favor? What are you talking about?"

"You gave me a push toward what I knew I wanted. I was afraid to take that step, afraid I'd disappoint all of us, afraid of the risk. But after I talked to you and thought about all the ways hiring you could be good for business, I got excited about trying it. I stopped being afraid before you ever walked in the door that first morning. And I was right! Don't you think this has been a good partnership?"

"It's been great. I'm having fun at work—who would have thought *that* might happen? And I'm learning the business. I like that there's more to learn than I realized. I'm forever grateful that you took the risk to take me on."

"Good! Then I think we need to talk about the next steps to take. I think it's time to hire someone else, to begin with. Your time is too valuable for some of what you're doing. Someone else could deliver those business orders, and I could use you here at lunchtime, for example. Chiffon, would you find and hire us an assistant for yourself? Could be a college student with a car or a mother with kids in school midday. Whatever you decide is fine with me. Let's write a job description and a preliminary schedule."

As she listened, Chiffon's early enthusiasm began to wane. Stan could see that something was wrong. Thinking that she might have been misjudging his intentions, he pressed on. "I'll stay out of the way. This will be yours to manage."

They were both quiet for a minute before Chiffon said, "Stan, I appreciate your confidence in me, I really do." She didn't know how to continue. She exhaled loudly, throwing her hands out in a gesture of helplessness. "I cannot guarantee you that I'll come through for you when you need me. You know my situation. I've let you down more than once by failing to show."

He nodded but said nothing.

"I'd love to think that I can be what you want me to be, but I know that the time will come when I let you down in a big, unforgivable way. And you deserve better than that."

He looked at his hands for a minute and then raised his head, looking her in the eye. "Chiffon, I know why you're frightened at the thought of more responsibility. I certainly don't want to be the source of too much stress for you. But you're good at this; you have good instincts. And I know we can make it work. In the past, when you couldn't be here, Carrie was able to fill in enough to get us by. And in the future, we'll have your assistant to rely on until we have you back. I'd rather work with 'most' of Chiffon than 'all' of someone else. We can do this together."

She was shaking her head sadly. "Stan, that would be so unfair to you, to Carrie, to any new employee. I wish you could count on me, but I am historically unreliable. I'm sorry."

"In all the time you've worked here, how many days do you suppose you've been unable to do your part? What do you think? Ten? Fifteen? Twenty?"

"It's probably somewhere in there, and that's way too many," she said.

"Well, whatever it is, we can work toward your repaying that time by allowing *me* time off. I want to spend more time with my family. I want to be able to take a vacation now and then. I want to leave early and go to a soccer game!"

"How does it benefit the business if one of us is always among the missing?"

He laughed. "It won't be always; it'll be when one

of us chooses or needs to take time. Mostly, we'll be here building the business, learning, growing, making things happen! Come on, Chiffon! I need you to be my partner—I can't do all that alone!"

"And what about my moods? You know what it's like when I'm unfit company. How many Cals do you need me to alienate before we have no customers left?"

"That guy is a jerk, and I'm glad he's gone. Aren't you? The other customers are, I'll bet. You're right; we don't want that kind of thing happening every time you're not in a great mood. But it only happened once, and I can't say I'm sorry."

She grinned. "If I hadn't felt so lousy that day, it would have felt good to get rid of him. I don't miss him, that's for sure!"

"So, let's focus on bringing in new customers while keeping the old ones happy. We can do this, Chiffon. You know we can." His smile and his sincerity were convincing her.

"Stan, you would have to promise me that if it wasn't going the way you expected, you'd tell me. No hard feelings, you can always let me go. You don't owe me anything."

"Au contraire. I owe you more than you know, partner. Now, I have some new ideas. Want to hear them?"

Chiffon realized that she *did* want to hear his thoughts for the future of the deli. And she had some of her own to contribute. Despite her earlier misgivings, she was feeling some excitement about the venture. Maybe something *was* turning around for her. It felt good to think so.

Chapter 46

On the third Monday of November, the deli was unusually quiet, even for a holiday week. Chiffon was standing alone at the counter, chewing something, when Henry entered. She held out her open hand to him. "Grape?" she offered.

"No thanks. You're selling fruit here now?"

"Of course not, Henry. That would be, like, a healthy choice, and we can't have *that* now, can we?" She grinned at Stan as he came around the corner. "Stan wouldn't stand for that, would you?"

"Don't be a smart aleck, Chiffon. Our *un*healthy options pay your rent and mine. Don't bite the hand that feeds you"—he looked down at his hands—"not that anyone would want to do *that,* I suppose." They all laughed at the prospect. "What are your Thanksgiving plans, Henry?"

"The usual. I'll stay home for dinner."

"Not another one! What's with the two of you? Antiholiday or something? Staying home alone on

Thanksgiving is un-American!" He walked away shaking his head.

Chiffon laughed again. "Great timing. We had just had the same conversation when you walked in."

Henry shrugged. "I always like the holidays but from a distance. I like to see other people prepare and plan. That's enough of a holiday experience for me."

"That *does* sound like you, I guess." She was thoughtful for a few seconds. "I have an idea," she began.

"No, Chiffon. Don't go having *ideas* now. Nothing good could come from that."

"Wait, now, don't dismiss my ideas until you hear them at least. What if … what if I cook dinner for the two of us! Don't shake your head!" That's what he was doing as she talked. "Don't say no; just listen. I'd love to cook a little turkey with all the trimmings, but I'd never bother for just myself. You'd be doing me a favor if you agreed to come for dinner. Nothing fancy, just the two of us for turkey and gravy. You don't have to spend the day, just come in time for dinner. Come on, Henry. Think about it. It might even be fun!" As she warmed to the idea, she grew more excited, and he could see that she was already planning a menu in her head.

"Chiffon, two minutes ago, we were agreeing that neither of us wanted to make a big deal of Thanksgiving. Now you're talking about turkey and gravy. I don't want to put you out like that. And I can never reciprocate, since I don't actually cook. Thanks for the offer, but I think we should just stick to the first plan."

Now she was the one shaking her head. "Henry, you

wouldn't be putting me out. It really would be nice to cook a meal for someone else. It'll be very low-key, very casual. Come on—will you please come for Thanksgiving dinner?"

Why hadn't he just gone home tonight, skipped the deli for the week? He was feeling trapped now, with no good reason to refuse her. And, in truth, he would have visited his mother on Thanksgiving in the past and wouldn't be doing that this year. "Okay, Chiffon. I'll come for Thanksgiving dinner."

She looked so pleased he was almost sorry he'd hesitated. He'd think about the problems this presented later. Like what should he bring? Couldn't be food because that might interfere with her menu. Couldn't be wine because he didn't know what she liked or if she drank it. Couldn't be flowers because she might be allergic. *Later*, he reminded himself, *think about this later*.

"Thank you, Henry. You won't regret it. I'm a good cook when I want to be. Say four o'clock?"

"Okay. I'll see you Thursday at four."

One his way home, he tried to think of a way out of this but couldn't come up with one. He wasn't much of a guest, he thought, but he'd have to make an effort. It was nice of her to do this, and she didn't realize how uncomfortable he'd be. He'd just have to figure out how to get through it.

Thursday dawned bright but cold. Henry took his bike, something for which he was truly thankful, out for a long ride early in the day. The few people he saw waved and called hello, all in the holiday spirit, he supposed.

When he got home, he made hot coffee and sat with the newspaper, enjoying the leisurely pace of this particular weekday. So far, so good.

He had decided to bring her a fruit basket, remembering those grapes she was eating on Monday. On his way home the night before, he'd stopped at a supermarket to pick one up. He was amazed by the number of people shopping on Wednesday night! The wait to check out was long, and everyone seemed to be in a great hurry. He walked out with the cellophane wrapping of the fruit basket crinkling loudly, happy to be out of there.

Getting ready to leave on Thursday, he retrieved the fruit from his refrigerator. Now he worried that it was the wrong choice. Would she laugh at him, saying, "Henry! What am I supposed to do with *that*?"

Or maybe she already had enough fruit; she had those grapes after all. Or maybe she only liked grapes, not apples and oranges and whatever else was in there. Or maybe—*Okay, stop!* he thought. Nothing he could do about it now.

Chiffon answered the door at the first ring. "Happy Thanksgiving!" she said as she waved him inside. Henry noticed immediately that everything was neat and presentable, unlike his last and only visit there. He hadn't realized that he was worried about this until he felt the relief.

"Happy Thanksgiving to you," he responded, holding the fruit out to her. He felt much lighter once she had taken it.

"Well, thank you so much! I love fruit, and I'll be snacking on this all weekend!"

Check.

Further relieved, Henry let himself smile for the first time. "It smells really good in here." He nodded approvingly.

"I made an apple pie this morning before I put the turkey in. You're probably smelling everything from dinner through dessert. Come on into the kitchen with me while I finish up with dinner."

Henry left his jacket on the sofa as he walked through the house behind her. The kitchen was warm and cozy, the air smelling even better than it had in the entry. There was a tiny teak table with two chairs with striped seat cushions on them against the window on one side of the room. Chiffon had set two places, and a small vase held some cut flowers in the middle of the table.

Double check, Henry thought.

"The turkey is almost done, and the potatoes are cooked. I just need to mash them. We were going to have carrots, but they felt soft, so I'm substituting green beans because they're fresher." She held a bean up as she snapped the end off, as if to prove it. "Make yourself comfortable." She waved toward a chair across the counter from where she was working.

"Can I help?" Henry asked, hoping she'd decline, since he really knew nothing about cooking and would surely do it wrong.

"Thank you but no. Most everything is done now,

and besides, you told me you can't cook. I'm not taking a chance on Thanksgiving dinner with a rookie!"

He smiled his relief. "You're right about that. But I feel a little useless just sitting here watching you work."

"Well, then, there is one thing. I've already opened the wine. Would you pour some for us? There are glasses on the sideboard with the bottle."

"I'd be happy to pour some wine." He turned to find it. She had put two delicate glasses beside a nice bottle of Beaujolais, cork already removed. Unsure about the amount, Henry decided that half-full seemed like a good idea. Not too much, not too little. He brought the glasses to the counter and sat back in his chair. He didn't want her to think he drank too much, so he decided that he'd drink when she did. That way he wouldn't finish first.

Music was playing in the background—nice, something instrumental that he didn't have to think about. Chiffon was humming as she whisked flour into a pan of gravy. "I think Thanksgiving is my favorite holiday," she offered. "When I was a kid, we didn't really celebrate. My parents believed that you should be thankful for your blessings all the time, not just on one special day. It's a nice sentiment, that one, but they counted learning to do without and stern correction of our transgressions among our blessings. We were supposed to be thankful for parents who cared enough to see that we adhered to their strict code of behavior. I remember wishing that we could be thankful for pumpkin pie or cranberry sauce, just once." She smiled. "But now that it's up to me, I celebrate every holiday I can find."

Henry wasn't sure how to respond. This was nothing like his experience of Thanksgiving. Did she want to know that? "In my home, we liked to celebrate Thanksgiving. We did it quietly, in our own way. But we always shared a meal and enjoyed being together. And watched the parade, of course."

"The parade! Yes, the parade!" She skipped a little on her way to the refrigerator for more butter. "I love the parade! The first time I saw it, I could think of no higher aspiration than holding one of those ropes for a float. I got over that, but I still do love watching it," she enthused, pushing a small dish of mixed nuts in his direction. "It sounds like it was nice at your house."

When she didn't continue, he thought maybe he should add something of his own to the conversation. After a few moments, he asked, "So how did you learn to cook a turkey then?" Asking questions seemed like a good idea, guaranteed to keep her talking. And he was right. Before he knew it, she was setting the serving dishes on the table and carrying their wineglasses to it.

They continued to talk easily through the dinner, which he assured her was delicious. She could have done much less, and he still would have been impressed. But this was truly a beautiful meal, and he appreciated it. By the end, he was pleasantly full and relaxed. Until he noticed the time. It was after seven! How had so much time gone by? Now he felt that maybe he had overstayed his welcome and became anxious. He stood to help her clear the table, while she continued to chatter amicably. But now he kept one eye on the clock while they talked.

Chiffon wouldn't let him do the dishes and fixed him a big container of leftovers to take home. She met him at the door with it when he'd retrieved his jacket.

"I can't thank you enough, Chiffon," he said sincerely. "That was a wonderful Thanksgiving dinner." And he immediately began to feel uneasy. Knowing his discomfort, Chiffon reached up and hugged him lightly, putting him out of the misery of not knowing what to do at the door.

"I'm so glad you came. You really did do me a favor! That was fun. Let's do it again next year!"

He laughed. "Chiffon, I'll bet you don't even know what you're doing tomorrow, never mind next year. We'll talk about it later, much later! But I really do appreciate *this* year!"

When he got home and put away his jacket and his leftovers, Henry sat in his favorite reading chair and sighed. It was good to be home.

Chapter 47

Henry liked movies but preferred to watch them at home. So, he was slightly dismayed when Chiffon asked him to go with her to see some classic film that she loved. He'd made the mistake of saying he'd never seen it. He thought he should have learned a lesson from the bike experience. But then, that had not turned out so badly. So, he found himself rallying and agreeing to meet her at the theater.

The showing was to be a matinee on Saturday at four o'clock. He parked in the front of the lot at a quarter after three and was surprised to see so few other vehicles. He surmised that the early hour must account for it and got out of the car, locking it after him. A few steps away, he returned to be sure he had locked it. With few patrons around, he reasoned, there would be few witnesses to a crime, should one occur.

He entered the lobby and was immediately struck by the dim light. When his eyes adjusted, he made his way along the walls, studying the posters mounted there.

The concession booths offered the expected popcorn and candy, but to his surprise, much more. A moviegoer could buy beer or wine, pizza, chicken wings—any number of food items to bring into the theater. He hoped she wouldn't want to do that. She'd probably suggest it, he'd claim disinterest, she'd wheedle, he'd finally agree, and in the end, he'd wear some kind of sauce home on his shirt. Those accidents never seemed to happen to her, always to him.

There were upholstered benches along the periphery of the large room. He made his way to one toward the back, realizing that he was very early, and Chiffon would most likely come running in at the last minute. At best. Equally likely, she'd be late.

For a while, Henry studied the patterns in the dark carpet. Eventually, he noticed that several people were milling around the lobby, and he worried that the theater would fill before Chiffon arrived. There were multiple movies showing, and he didn't know what these others were there to see. So, he decided he'd best buy their tickets. He thought that an especially good idea, since she'd probably be late.

He followed a young couple to the line at the ticket booth and bought two tickets when it was his turn. He had no idea that movie tickets cost so much! But he'd probably never do it again, so he could justify the expense this one time.

He checked the time and sat back down to wait. He tapped his foot anxiously as he watched the double doors from the parking lot. Three fifty and no sign of her. He began to grow annoyed.

Three fifty-four and still no Chiffon.

At 3:58, one of the doors opened, and he began to stand but sat again when he saw that it wasn't her.

He was irritated that they'd miss the beginning of the film that *she* insisted he see. She really could be so inconsiderate!

At 4:12, he was pacing the lobby, unable to sit still.

At 4:20, he could no longer contain his annoyance, and he walked briskly out the door and headed for his car. The morning had been overcast, and now it threatened to rain. He angrily tossed the two tickets on the passenger seat after unlocking the car. When he got in, he retrieved them and tucked them neatly into his wallet and drove home. There was no excuse for her behavior, and he could hardly wait to tell her about it!

But wait he did. He waited until Monday and his normal stop at the deli. If she didn't say anything about it, neither would he. And then when he handed her his money, he'd slip the ticket on top of the bills and just wait for her reaction. When she saw the ticket and was reminded, she'd be enormously apologetic. And he'd hold out on forgiving her. After all, she needed to understand how unacceptable it was.

But she wasn't there when he entered the deli. It was busy and somewhat chaotic. Stan was rushing around and adding to the chaos. She should have been there, and Henry felt worry creeping into his thoughts. Where was she? Was something wrong?

When Stan saw him waiting at the counter, he motioned him back toward the kitchen. Henry had never been back there and thought, briefly, that Stan meant to put him to work. Instead, Stan turned to him and said, "Henry, I don't know if you're aware of what happened, but maybe you could talk to Doreen here …" He motioned to a woman sitting on a folding chair in a corner of the room. "Doreen, Henry is a friend of Chiffon's, and maybe he can help you." Stan looked overwrought but also like he had just escaped something as he hurried back to the front of the store.

Henry stared at the stranger. There was something familiar about her, but only in a distant kind of way. Her face reminded him of Chiffon's but with much more animation and, well, lack of control. Funny that he should have such a thought about "Chiffon" and "control" at the same time, he thought. Then the woman was out of her chair and upon him.

"Do you have *any* idea what is happening? Do you know what they could possibly expect of me? Why, why would she have them contact *me*, of all people?" She stood right in front of him, and he could feel the electricity spitting from her as she shifted from foot to foot, eyes wide and frantic.

For his part, Henry was completely at a loss. What on earth was she talking about? Who were *they*, and how was he supposed to know what was going on here? They stared at each other for a few seconds until he said, "I have no idea what you mean!" *Truer words were never spoken*, he thought. But whatever it was, he was feeling increasingly uneasy about it.

"You mean you don't know? Well, I don't know why

Stan thinks you can help me when you don't even know what happened yet! You want to know? You want to know what happened?" She paced quickly before him in the small space, eyes casting about as if for the answers that he didn't have. Not waiting for a reply, she continued, "I'll tell you what happened. The police found Chiffon on the floor in her basement. She was unresponsive, and they've taken her to a hospital. And they keep asking *me* questions about her—about her medical condition and habits and all manner of things that I can't possibly know. Why, why would they ask *me* anything? Why do they think I know anything?" If it was possible, she seemed to be getting more agitated as the seconds went by.

Somewhere around the word "police," a gray fog began to creep into Henry's consciousness. It grew as she continued to talk, or rant, at him. He felt heat in his ears and heard a buzzing in his head. By the time she finished, he was leaning against a large refrigerator door and slowly sinking toward a sitting position on the floor. "I'm so sorry," he finally managed. "Are you Chiffon's sister?"

"Haven't you been listening at all? Good lord, are you sure you're a friend of hers? Yes! Yes, I'm her sister. They called me Saturday afternoon, and I flew in from Baltimore early Sunday. And now they expect me to become involved for some reason!"

He watched her continue to pace and rant as if through thick lenses. He couldn't quite focus on what she was saying. But he caught the gist of it: accident, hospital, prognosis unknown. After a few minutes, he slowly stood. He brushed off his clothes and cleared his throat. She stopped talking long enough for him to ask, "Can you tell me where she is?"

She looked at him as if he'd just asked her to remove her head. "Are you kidding me? You are unbelievable! You don't listen at all!" She leaned in closely and spoke very slowly and loudly, "She's. In. The. Hospital."

Normally, Henry would have bristled at such treatment, but he was too befuddled and anxious right now to muster the energy for that. He just stared at her until she raked her hands through her hair and said, "You must know each other from some sort of program or something. She's always had problems and is always trying some new 'solution' or other. That must be it." She reached into her pocket as a light dawned and pulled out a folded piece of paper. "Then maybe you know what *this* is all about!" She tossed the paper to him. "They said she was holding this when they found her. Explain *that* to me, if you can!"

He unfolded the paper slowly and saw Chiffon's handwriting on the page. He read:

The thickness of time

A glance outside and the sky looks weary,
yet patient, and the clouds! those clouds
are like blotchy, aching bruises against
its pale blue white flesh and the trees
are stretched across it poised to scratch
and draw rain from the pinkish horizon
except that now it gets darker and the

branches blur and only brush the sky, not sharp enough anymore to hurt it but that doesn't matter because its anguish is complete and now, tonight, it tries to weep, to display its soft and fleshy pain but little happens; a meager, dispersed mist is the best it can do and even that dries almost immediately and is forgotten even sooner because no one notices and even if they did, so what? no one can do anything and they wouldn't if they could but then it gets darker still and the sky quiets, pausing in its manner of apology before the moon which rises and, rather than be a comfort, burns a fuzzy hole in its paper-thin texture, a hole through which it bleeds pale illumination on a beneath-the-sky that might be better off left in the dark.

A glance inside and the room is full of confusing angles and sharp lines like carved diamond or ice or maybe tin cans emptied of baby peas or whole kernel corn and they break it up into little pieces that can never be put back together unless they are melted by a great heat but no heat seems to be present at all in this room which is as tight as a stretched rubber band and everything—furniture, walls,

> me—can't help but collapse and fold into a neat flat package because it's all so sharp and stiff like brittle wire-gone-haywire but the window! the window with its panes of solid nothing (emptiness is something but there's nothing to it), at least it holds the innards in place, not that they have anywhere to go except the sky which has its own misery to blunt and would crack under the strain if not for the soft gullies made by nail-bitten fingers; the room is fragile and it splinters easily and continually falls into place, its place being fallen.

Henry could not begin to make sense of this. But it felt like part of Chiffon, and he felt like a voyeur for even reading it. There was an urgency now to protect this small part of her from any other prying eyes, especially those of her sister. He began to fold the paper into an ever-smaller whole. If she questioned him, he'd say it was a nervous habit. No doubt she'd buy that excuse. But she didn't question it, had gone off into another rant, and didn't see him slip it into his pocket.

Trying to compose himself, Henry also began to pace, and now the small space was impossible. He nodded quickly at her and left the kitchen. Out front, Stan looked a little frantic when he saw Henry moving toward the door. "Henry! Everything okay?"

But Henry just kept walking.

Chapter 48

The week had been trying for Chiffon. Things were going well at the deli, and she felt good about the job she was doing. But there was this restlessness that she just couldn't seem to soothe. It happened, of course, from time to time. She wondered why, with all her experience, she didn't know how to better deal with it.

It was Saturday morning, and she was having trouble getting herself moving for the day. She knew that she'd meet Henry at the theater later, and that was *something* to look forward to. But, for now, there was this restlessness.

The Big Question was driving her right now. The Big Question, for Chiffon, was "Who am I?" She had struggled with this her entire adult life. It seemed like a simple question, but she could not for the life of her begin to answer it. It was as if someone else had the answer and if she showed that person the right version of Chiffon she'd get that answer. Chameleonlike, she changed her presentation to accommodate what she thought everyone else expected to see. It was exhausting, this constant stream of masks and behavior changes. And, maddeningly, she had no idea which was the real Chiffon. If such a thing existed.

Because she couldn't answer the question of *who*, the answer to the *where* also eluded her. She felt like she had never belonged. Anywhere. She had a great number of acquaintances and was part of many groups. But in none of them did she feel like she belonged, like she was home. They were all wrong in some way. She was not being selective about it; it was an instinctual thing. She just never felt a real part of any of them.

And without the who or the where, she couldn't uncover her true purpose. Chiffon believed that everyone had true purposes and that most people didn't try to reveal them. But it was important for her to know. In no way old, she still felt the weight of her days now. She needed to know her purpose while she could still hope to accomplish it.

So she made a cup of tea and sat down in her everyday world to write something for the Blue Book. An hour or so later, she finished and noticed the time. *I should hurry,* she thought, *before Carl gets here to fix that dripping faucet.* She had asked a neighbor to take a look at the kitchen plumbing and fix it for her. He said he'd stop by late Saturday morning, and it was nearly eleven.

She opened the door and stepped into the basement stairway, thinking about a promise she'd made to the animal shelter staff. On the third step down, something in her brain opened up. Some wall that was necessary was suddenly gone. In a flash of shiny, blinding black, Chiffon stepped over the brink.

Later, authorities would conclude that she fell down the stairs (what dumb luck!) and hit her head when she landed at the bottom, causing the brain injury. In fact, the brilliant black explosion in her brain caused her to become completely unaware of the stairs or anything else around her. By the time her body came to rest at the bottom, she was already beyond feeling pain of any kind in it.

When Carl arrived a short time later, he entered with the key she had given him, thinking that she wasn't home. He noticed the open door and a light in the stairwell. He walked toward it and began to call, "Chi—" Before her name left his lips, he saw her. He dialed 911 on his way down the stairs.

Chapter 49

Henry brought the trash cans into the garage and walked back down the driveway. He looked around the yard, searching out damage from the morning's storm. It had been a busy day, but he had checked most things off his Saturday list. He picked up some bits of debris and righted some of his flowers, shaking the mud off as he did. He became aware that he was hearing a small noise and that it kept repeating itself. He walked back to the end of the driveway and stood watching the boy in the street. It was the youngest one, the one who always followed the group and then came home alone when he couldn't catch up.

He was trying to ride his bike down the street, but the chain slipped off every time he began to pedal. So Henry was hearing *whirr*, *chink*—pause while he tried to put it back on the gear—*whirr*, *chink*, pause.

After watching for another minute, Henry sighed and called out, "Bring it over here."

The boy looked around, as if there was someone else

he might be addressing. Seeing no one, he brought his hand up slowly and pointed at himself with a questioning look on his face.

"Yes, you. Bring your bike over here." He was trying to be patient, but the kid made it difficult.

The boy hesitated before beginning to walk slowly toward him. Henry turned and went into the garage, waving for the boy to follow. When he finally got there, Henry reached for the bike. The boy shoved it toward him, taking a step back at the same time. Henry shook his head and turned the bike over on his workbench. He waved the boy to the other side so he could watch. After making a small adjustment, he put the chain back on and spun the pedal. He looked at the boy to make sure he was watching, and then he took it off again. He repeated the actions, not saying a word but wanting the kid to know how to fix it himself next time. Then he put the bike back on the floor and wheeled it out to the street, where he handed it off. The boy got on and looped back and forth across the street a couple of times, grinning all the while. "Thanks, mister!" he yelled as he sped away, spraying sandy water from the wet road in his wake.

As he turned the key in the ignition and prepared to back down the driveway, Henry thought Chiffon would have loved to see *that*.

Fifteen minutes later, he parked and hurried toward the building, realizing that he'd planned to arrive earlier.

The doors whispered closed behind him, and he waved to the receptionist at the front desk, walking briskly past the elevators to the stairs. When he reached the fourth floor, he turned right to room 417, about halfway down the corridor. He knocked and entered quickly as Janice was about to begin dinner.

She looked up and smiled. "Henry! Was thinking we weren't going to see you tonight after all."

He shook his head and shook his jacket off at the same time. "Just a little delayed, Janice. I'm ready to take over." As she was about to leave the room, he called, "Wait! Janice, this is so disappointing." He nodded toward the dinner tray. "How many times do I have to explain that she doesn't like tapioca? Who do I have to talk to?"

The woman sighed as she took the small bowl from the tray. "I'm sorry, Henry. I know—you have told us, but special requests like that are easy to overlook. And, honestly, she eats it like everything else."

"Of course she does! She doesn't have much choice, does she? But I *know* she doesn't like it, so please try to see that she gets some other dessert, okay?" He made a mental note to bring it up *again* at the next care plan meeting with the staff.

Janice left with the tapioca, and he leaned in and asked conspiratorially, "Well? What do you think? Have we solved that? No, I don't think we have, either." Chiffon didn't respond. She didn't ever respond. But Henry acted as if she might at any time. It was the only way he could seem to talk to her. "Now, let's see what else you have for dinner tonight … Ah, looks good!" And he began to feed her small amounts, pausing between bites to give her time to swallow and, he hoped, enjoy it. He smiled his approval when Janice returned with a small cup of ice cream. "Thank you," he said as she waved and left the room. To Chiffon, he said, "Ice cream tonight! Your favorite!"

When they were finished and he had pushed the dinner cart aside, he sat back and looked out the window. Without looking at her, he said, "This was a dreary day, wasn't it? Seems like it's been raining for weeks. Supposed to be nice tomorrow, though."

He went to his jacket and took something from a pocket. He sat back down and smiled at her. "I have a surprise for you. I thought you could use something to take you away from the rain and gray sky." He held up a small piece of a pine branch and brought it to her nose as he crushed some needles together with his thumb and index finger. "I brought you a beautiful summer day." And he wondered if he saw the smallest flicker of light in her eyes.

Acknowledgments

I am so very fortunate to have had the support of a number of wonderful people in this endeavor. My chief readers and biggest fans, Ken Knox, husband, and Joanne Audette, sister—I couldn't have done it without you.

Many others contributed in large ways and small. Kathy, Tanya, Jennifer, Josie and Bill, Tyler, Christie, Skip, Oliver, Rick, Wendy, Aidan, Chelsie—I could go on. I appreciate all your support.

A sincere thank-you to the Robert Gammons Permanent Lending Library, Literary Department.

And for those nudges that I needed along the way—thank you to Matt Laliberte, Maribeth McNair, and Fred Ivor-Campbell.

Made in the USA
Lexington, KY
04 August 2018